The Secret of the Old Rifle

CROSSWAY BOOKS BY STEPHEN BLY

THE STUART BRANNON WESTERN SERIES

Hard Winter at Broken Arrow Crossing
False Claims at the Little Stephen Mine
Last Hanging at Paradise Meadow
Standoff at Sunrise Creek
Final Justice at Adobe Wells
Son of an Arizona Legend

THE NATHAN T. RIGGINS WESTERN
ADVENTURE SERIES
(Ages 9–14)

The Dog Who Would Not Smile
Coyote True
You Can Always Trust a Spotted Horse
The Last Stubborn Buffalo in Nevada
Never Dance with a Bobcat
Hawks Don't Say Goodbye

THE CODE OF THE WEST SERIES

It's Your Misfortune & None of My Own
One Went to Denver & the Other Went Wrong
Where the Deer & the Antelope Play
Stay Away From That City . . . They Call It Cheyenne
My Foot's in the Stirrup . . . My Pony Won't Stand

THE AUSTIN-STONER FILES

The Lost Manuscript of Martin Taylor Harrison
The Final Chapter of Chance McCall

THE LEWIS AND CLARK SQUAD ADVENTURE SERIES
(Ages 9–14)

Intrigue at the Rafter B Ranch
The Secret of the Old Rifle
Treachery at the River Canyon

BOOK TWO

The Secret of the Old Rifle

STEPHEN BLY

CROSSWAY BOOKS • WHEATON, ILLINOIS
A DIVISION OF GOOD NEWS PUBLISHERS

The Secret of the Old Rifle

Copyright © 1997 by Stephen Bly

Published by Crossway Books
　　　　a division of Good News Publishers
　　　　1300 Crescent Street
　　　　Wheaton, Illinois 60187

Cover illustration: Sergio Giovine

Cover design: Cindy Kiple

First printing, 1997

Printed in the United States of America

Library of Congress Cataloging-in-Publication Data
Bly, Stephen, 1944-
　　The secret of the old rifle / Stephen Bly.
　　　　p.　　cm.—(The Lewis & Clark Squad adventure series ; bk. 2)
　　Summary: When the Squad tries to solve the mystery of a cryptic
note found in the stock of an old rifle, they learn something about
God's justice and human friendship.
　　ISBN 0-89107-940-8
　　[1. Friendship—Fiction.　2. Christian life—Fiction.　3. Mystery
and detective stories.]　I. Title. II. Series: Bly, Stephen A.,
1944-　　Lewis & Clark Squad adventure series　;　bk. 2.
PZ7.B6275Se 1997
[F]—dc21　　　　　　　　　　　　　　　　　　　96-40081

05		04		03		02		01		00		99		98		97
15	14	13	12	11	10	9	8	7	6	5	4	3	2	1

For my good pal
Lane Ailor

One

◐

Quick! It's over here!" Larry Lewis shouted in his high-pitched, excited voice.

Cody Clark sprinted across the dimly lit basement. The heels of his cowboy boots slammed into the concrete at each step. "It's coming your way, Townie!"

"It turned! It turned!" Jeremiah Yellowboy hollered. He rubbed his fingers over his short black hair. "Where did it go?"

"Here it comes!" Larry shrieked.

Cody heard a loud slap of a plastic bat pounding the concrete. He zipped around a stack of dusty newspapers.

"I missed it!" Larry groaned, his University of Indiana tank top hanging off one shoulder, his blond hair in his eyes.

"Don't kill it," Feather Trailer-Hobbs thundered. "I've got a shoe box. We can trap it in the box and take it out-side!" She balanced herself on an empty crate and towered above the boys even more than normal.

"Set your bats to stun!" Cody commanded.

Jeremiah, with a grin as wide as his round cheeks, faked a salute. "Aye, aye, Captain Clark!"

"Where did it go?" Larry quizzed.

"It's over here," Cody yelled. "Hey . . . there's two of them!" A large flying furball rocketed past him. Cody's tennis racket caught the squirrel in mid-jump. The charcoal gray rodent smashed into the cement wall of the Yellowboy basement. When it dropped to the dusty floor, it didn't move.

"I got one!" Cody boomed. "Did you see that? And that was my backhand. Even Aggasi couldn't return that! Scoop him up, Feather."

"Andre Aggasi or the squirrel?" Jeremiah teased.

"Is he dead?" Feather asked, slowly approaching the motionless rodent.

"Stunned." Cody gritted his slightly crooked teeth and tried not to smile. "He's just stunned."

"Severely stunned. Maybe even fatally stunned," Jeremiah laughed.

"Don't touch it!" Larry hollered. "Sort of rake it up. They can give you rabies. Man, we don't want anyone sick. We have a basketball game tonight."

Jeremiah dashed to the back of the basement. "There goes the other one!"

Cody caught sight of movement to his left. "Get him, Larry!"

A piercing scream brought both boys running toward Larry's end of the junk-filled, dusty basement.

"What happened?" Cody shouted.

"He ran up my leg!" Larry screamed as he danced around stomping both feet.

Jeremiah raised the shovel handle over his head. "Which leg? Hold still."

"Not now! I shook him out. . . . He's over there—by that trunk." He tossed down the plastic bat and headed for the stairs.

"Where are you going?" Cody asked.

"To get something!" Larry took the wooden stairs two at a time.

"I think you killed this one," Feather called out from the other side of the room. "It's not breathing or anything."

"Over here, Cody!" Jeremiah pointed.

Cody hollered, "There it is! It ran behind the water heater!"

Jeremiah positioned the shovel handle above his head. "Can you reach it?"

"I can't get a good swing. Townie, I'll chase it out on your side. Ready?"

"Ready."

Cody stared at the squirrel's beady black eyes.

Lord, this is not working! Are You sure this is the way You wanted me to spend my morning?

"Well?" Jeremiah questioned.

"He won't run."

"What do you mean, he won't run?"

On his hands and knees, Cody poked the tennis racket behind the water heater. "He wants to fight. He won't run."

Feather stood behind Cody, a blue shoe box in her hand. "How do you know it's a he?"

"He, she—who cares!" Jeremiah called out. "It's eating the insulation out of our walls! We've trapped that squirrel four times. We turned him loose in the city park, and all four times he's eaten his way back into the basement. We've got to get rid of it somehow. Throw something at it."

Cody searched around quickly for something small. "There's nothing to throw!"

Out of the corner of his eye he saw Feather toss something at the gray squirrel cowering behind the hot water heater.

"What did you throw?" he asked.

"My gum."

"Well, the squirrel just ate it."

"Used licorice gum? Gross!" Jeremiah groaned. "That ought to kill it!"

"I wonder if that's considered cruel and unusual punishment?" Cody laughed, still looking for something to toss.

"Very funny! The squirrel obviously has better taste than some people I know!"

Cody turned and flipped open a big olive green trunk behind him. *Guns and bullets? Nope, I don't think I'll throw those.*

He reached into his jeans and pulled out a few coins. The first penny hit in front of the squirrel, and the animal didn't even flinch. The second one bounced off the squirrel's haunches, but the rodent kept its steely gaze fixed on Cody.

"Oh, man, I hate to do this." Cody gripped a quarter in his hand. He sailed the two-bit piece like a miniature Frisbee. It struck the squirrel below the ear, and the bushy-tailed rodent flashed past Jeremiah Yellowboy.

The shovel handle crashed and vibrated like a fast ball hitting a baseball bat tight on the wrists. "Oh! I missed him!"

Cody, still on his hands and knees, peeked around the water heater. "He's headed toward the stairs!"

"Head him off, Cody!" Jeremiah cried out. "Try to keep him in the center of the room!"

"Me? I'm way over here." He glanced up at Feather's long brown ponytail. "Feather, you'll have to—"

Like a doomsday planet hurled through outer space, the spinning orange globe rushed downward toward the fleeing rodent at twice the speed of sound. Unaware of impending doom, the squirrel paused briefly to survey his attackers and plot his escape route. It proved to be a fatal mistake.

At approximately 10:34 A.M. . . . at 810 First Street . . . in Halt, Idaho . . . about halfway between the "Rawlings RLW Wide Channel" markings and the "inflate 7-9 lbs" . . . the orange dimples of the "NCAA Final Four, indoor/outdoor" basketball struck the gray squirrel directly on top of its tiny-brained head.

"I got it!" Larry shouted from the top of the basement stairs. "Was that a good throw or what? I'm the best there ever was!"

Jeremiah, Feather, and Cody scurried over to examine what was left of the wreckage.

"How is it?" Larry shouted.

"I don't think it's stunned either," Feather replied.

"Now that is really gross!" Jeremiah groaned. "Dribbled to death. What a way to go."

"Nice toss, Larry. The squirrel has gone to his eternal rest," Cody reported.

"Squirrel? But how's my basketball?"

Feather squinted her eyes, wrinkled her thin nose, and frowned at Larry Lewis. "Your basketball?"

"Yeah, that's my favorite outdoor ball."

"It has a gray smudge on it." Jeremiah dribbled it around the concrete basement floor. "But I don't think it's seriously damaged."

"I can't believe you are more concerned with your basketball than you are this poor squirrel," Feather groused.

"I figure we just saved it from a slow, painful death from overeating fiberglass insulation," Cody argued.

Feather turned her back. "Well, it's smushed, and I'm not picking it up."

Cody scooped the squirrel up on the tennis racket with the toe of his boot and then dropped it into the shoe box alongside the other one. "All right, Townie, mission accomplished," he reported. "You can tell your mother she won't be bothered with squirrels in the basement anymore."

"At least not those two," Larry said as he leaped down the stairs. "Are there any more down here?"

"I don't think so. My brother patched the hole in the wall where they chewed their way in." Jeremiah searched the basement corners just in case.

Cody retreated to the water heater and dropped down to his hands and knees. The floor was cold and gritty. The whole room smelled musty.

"What are you doing?" Larry asked.

"Trying to get my quarter back."

"You threw money at it?"

"Yeah," Jeremiah droned, "he tried to buy it off, but the squirrel wanted ten bucks!"

"So you threw a quarter?" Larry pressed.

Cody dragged the tennis racket handle across the concrete until the quarter was within reach. "It beats tossing bullets at it."

"Bullets?" Feather jammed the lid tight on the shoe box.

"I was looking for something to throw and opened that trunk. There are guns and bullets in there."

"Oh, yeah." Jeremiah grinned. "That stuff belongs to my grandfather. He got it from his father. Come here. . . . Look at this gun. It is so cool."

"I don't like guns," Feather announced.

Cody stared at her gray-green eyes and the tiny earrings in her double-pierced ears.

How can she look me in the eyes and turn her nose up at the same time?

"But this is an antique. It's like looking at history," Jeremiah announced. "My grandpa says this Winchester '73 rifle was used during the Nez Perce Indian War in 1877." He gingerly pulled out the gun.

"By the Indians, right?" Larry quizzed.

Jeremiah sighed. "You one smart paleface."

Unfazed, Larry asked, "Does it still work?"

"Oh, yeah. My grandad likes to hunt with it when he comes down to see me."

"Is it loaded?"

Jeremiah checked the lever. Both Feather and Larry jumped back a step.

"Nope. See . . . the chamber's empty. Grandpa keeps his old carbine at his house and his rifle here. That way he can hunt at either place."

"What's the difference between a rifle and a carbine?" Larry asked.

"The carbine barrel's about four inches shorter than this rifle."

"Yeah," Cody interrupted, "they used the carbines horseback. They usually had a saddle ring mounted on the left side. That way you could tie it to your saddle. But this is a rifle. It's used for longer shots."

"How about all those brass tacks on the wood? What do they do?" Feather asked.

"Oh, that's just some fancy decorations my great-great-grandfather put on."

"I don't even know who my great-great-grandfather was," Feather admitted, "and you have some of the things that belonged to yours. That is so awesome."

"Yeah . . . well . . . there are some days I really like being Nez Perce. Then other days I wish I was somebody else."

"This isn't the gun called a yellowboy, is it?" Larry asked. "You told us once that your last name came from the yellowboy rifle. But there isn't much brass on this one."

"It's the '66 Winchester that's called a yellowboy. This is a '73. A '66 has this metal part in the middle—called a receiver—all in brass, just like this piece on the bottom," Jeremiah informed them.

"Wow, that is yellow." Feather rubbed the smooth, mirrorlike brass on the carrier. Then she examined the back of the stock of the gun Jeremiah held in his hand. "Hey, there's a little brass button back here. What does that do?"

"Oh, you slide that over, and it opens a compartment where the cleaning rods are stored." Jeremiah shoved the brass button to the right and held the rifle up, allowing the three wooden rods to slip out. "You don't find many '73s that still have the original rods like this one."

"That's cool—a secret compartment!" Feather's smile revealed the slight gap between her two front teeth.

"Well, it's not secret." Cody shrugged. "Most all the old Winchesters have them."

"Are we going to practice basketball or what?" Larry spun the ball on the middle finger of his right hand.

"Not until after Cody has a funeral for the squirrels," Feather replied.

"A what?"

"We all know that you talk to the Lord all the time. Besides, we can't just toss them into the forest."

"Why not?"

"Well . . . we clobbered them. We ought to bury them. Animals have rights, too." She patted the top of the shoe box.

"But not rites! I figured we'd treat the coyotes or the owls to a free meal. Isn't that being nice to animals?" Cody suggested.

"Bring a shovel, Jeremiah," she ordered. "We are going to have a burial, and Cody's going to pray over them."

"But there's no squirrel heaven," Cody protested.

"How do you know?"

Feather, Cody, and Larry began to stroll toward the stairs.

"Wait a minute, guys," Jeremiah called out. "Cody, help me get these rods in here. . . . They don't want to go back in."

Cody tried sliding the rods into the hole in the back of the rifle one at a time, but the third one jammed tight. "Is that the way they go?"

"I've never had any trouble before."

"Well . . . something's jammed down in there."

"Probably hidden jewels!" Feather exclaimed.

"Probably dirt," Larry countered.

Jeremiah poured the other two rods back out into Cody's waiting hands. "Can you see anything in there?"

"A black hole," Cody reported. "Hold it by the light."

They stepped over to the uncovered seventy-five watt lightbulb. Jeremiah held the rifle by the barrel, and Cody peeked inside.

"Do you see anything?"

"Not really."

"Maybe we need a flashlight," Feather suggested.

"Come on, guys, it's already late. I've got our basketball practice all organized," Larry pressured. "By now we should be on Pick and Roll #6."

Feather grimaced. "What are Pick and Roll #1, 2, 3, 4, and 5?"

"See? That's exactly why we need more practice. You guys did memorize those plays I gave you yesterday, didn't you?"

"You said it was to be a short practice today because of our game tonight," Cody reminded him.

"Right, right. Just a dozen of the fundamentals and then . . ."

A united glare from Cody, Feather, and Jeremiah silenced Larry.

"Go get that blue flashlight on the workbench." Jeremiah motioned. "There's something stuck down there."

"Maybe it's a bullet," Cody guessed. "Maybe someone thought that's how you load it. My brother once had a little .22 that loaded through the stock." He picked up the light and once again peered into the half-inch diameter round hole.

"Whoa! There it is!" Cody exclaimed.

"What is it?" Jeremiah queried.

"A cleaning patch . . . or maybe a wad of paper."

Larry dribbled the basketball around on the concrete basement floor. "Well, pull it out. Let's go practice."

Cody wiggled his finger into the hole. "I can't reach it."

"It could be a treasure map to a lost gold mine or something," Feather suggested. "If it is, we have to split it four ways."

"Four ways? It's my grandad's rifle!"

"All right, five ways," she conceded. "Is it a deal?"

Cody scooped up a wire coat hanger from the floor and began to untwist it. "What do you want with one-fifth of a gold mine?"

"I'd buy myself a big house."

"I thought you were going to make big money off that Pizza Palace commercial," Larry remarked.

Feather tilted her head and skewed her face sideways. "Bruce said that—"

"Oh, now you've dropped the Baxter and just call him Bruce?" Cody chided.

She stuck out her tongue. "He told me to call him Bruce. And he said I had a lot of untapped potential. So there! But he said I would only make money if they decide to use that scene. If not, I only get a measly fifty bucks."

"I wouldn't mind having fifty bucks." Larry stopped dribbling and hugged the basketball under his arms. "That would fix my backboard, and then we wouldn't have to practice at the barn."

Feather looked down at her canvas basketball shoes. "I like it out there."

Cody picked up some pliers from the workbench and straightened the coat hanger. Then he bent a small fish-hook at the end. "All right, let's see if this works." He shoved the wire into the open hole at the end of the rifle stock. "There we go. . . . Got it."

A wad of yellowed paper tumbled to the floor. Cody slipped the rods back into place. Jeremiah slid the small door closed and returned the rifle to the trunk.

Feather shoved the box of demised squirrels at Larry and swooped up the piece of faded yellow paper. She carefully unwrapped it and held it up.

"There's some writing on it," she announced.

"My great-grandfather's name was Ezekiel," Jeremiah told her. "Does it say Ezekiel Yellowboy?"

"Nope." She moved a little closer to the lightbulb. "It's written in pencil, so it's hard to read. I think it says, 'God is just.'"

"God is just?" Larry choked. "You mean like on that concrete tombstone we discovered last week out near the creek behind Eureka Blaine's corrals?"

"There's a kind of formula and then 'God is just.'"

"Formula? Let me see." Cody held his hand out.

"Don't you believe me?"

"Of course we believe you." Cody sighed. "I'd just like to read it for myself."

Jeremiah scooted behind Cody and attempted to spy over his shoulder, but Cody stood four inches taller.

Cody held the note up to the light. "'God is just' . . ."

"I already told you that," Feather huffed.

"'$A + B + C + D =$ God is just.'"

"What kind of equation is that?" Larry shoved the box of squirrels back over to Feather.

"Maybe there are A, B, C, and D graves out at Blaine's! We can take a look when we get out to Cody's ranch," Jeremiah proposed.

"Not until after basketball practice," Larry persisted. "This is the second week of summer three-on-three, and we've already lost one game."

"And not until after the squirrel burial," Feather added, waving the blue shoe box at them.

"I better leave this note with the rifle." Jeremiah sauntered back over to the trunk. "I think I'll call Grandad and ask him if he knows what it means."

All four scrambled up the stairs out of the basement.

"'A + B + C + D = God is just,'" Cody repeated. "In a rifle? Does it mean someone used the gun to carry out God's justice?"

"Ah, hah! The secret of the rifle! Another unsolved mystery for the bold, fearless, and daring Lewis and Clark Squad," Jeremiah whooped. "Hey . . . don't turn out the light until I get to the top of the stairs! This basement can get really, really dark and scary."

Two

❖

*A*ctually, Pick and Roll #6 worked very well.

When the score reached twelve to four, Cody figured they had the game won. Of course, it did help that the Eastside Rowdies had to do without the services of Randy Severe. Randy was in the eighth grade, stood six-foot-two, weighed 250 pounds, and had a vertical leap of about one-half inch—tops. He could pull down most rebounds due to his height, and the fact that no one dared jump over his back to reach the ball. Besides that, Randy had a nice, soft set shot from anywhere in the paint.

But Randy was in California visiting his grandmother, and Cody was left to guard Speed Steinbeck. That was much easier, especially since Speed spent most of his time wanting to visit with Feather—even when she sat on the bench waiting to get into the game.

Finally, Speed was kicked in the rear end by Tom V. Deedorf, captain of the Rowdies. Tom V. was a cousin to Tom B. Deedorf, who played on the Camas Combines. At that point the game got a little more competitive.

It was Larry Lewis who drove to the basket, pulled back, and tossed up a little twelve-foot jumper to score the game-winning bucket.

Twenty to twelve.

"All right! Two wins and only one loss. Now we have a winning record. Let's keep it that way!"

After customary fives to the Rowdies, the Lewis and Clark Squad huddled near the front door of the gym.

"I think I saw J. J. Melton outside in the parking lot," Jeremiah warned.

Feather grabbed Cody's arm. "Is he still trying to beat you up just because you made him stop teasing me?"

"I haven't seen him since they all came out to the barn last week. It's like he's been avoiding me. Kind of nice actually," Cody admitted.

"Maybe your brother Denver talked to him," Feather suggested.

"I don't think so. . . . I told Denver this was something I needed to settle on my own."

"Well," Larry put in, "a little help from your friends never hurt, did it?"

Cody studied Larry's bright blue eyes. "What do you mean, help from my friends?"

"Eh . . . nothing, really." Larry shrugged. "Let's all go to my house. I've got a case of Mountain Dew in the downstairs refrigerator."

They plowed out of the gym and across the gravel parking lot. J. J. Melton and Rocky Hammers loitered on the concrete steps next to the Coke machine. Cody stopped, half expecting them to shout something. Instead, they just turned away and gazed out at the prairie.

He poked Jeremiah. "Does it seem strange for J. J. and Rocky to keep quiet? You don't suppose they've suddenly become more mature, do you?"

Both boys paused for a moment and then broke out in wide grins. "No way!" they echoed.

Cody tugged at Larry's sweaty tie-dyed T-shirt. "Whoa! What exactly did you mean about help from my friends? What did you do to J. J.?"

"Me?" Larry said wide-eyed. "I'm a wimp when it comes to throwing punches. You know that."

"I didn't ask if you punched him. I asked what you did."

"Hey, it's no big deal. It's nothing you wouldn't have done for me."

The four tramped through the cottonwood-shaded city park, past the swings, and down onto the gravel lane called Third Avenue. Thick white clouds floated by seemingly just above the treetops. The breeze dried Cody's sweaty sleeveless T-shirt.

"Come on, Lewis, what did you do?"

"Well . . . I just gave them a little warning."

"A little warning?" Jeremiah pried. "You didn't call them out, did you? Oh, man, tell me you didn't call them out."

"There's four of us and only three of them," Feather pointed out. "Maybe we could take them."

"Sure, if they had their hands tied behind their backs

and we were allowed to use guns and knives." Jeremiah sighed. "What did you do, Larry?"

"All I did was tell them that if they hassled us one more time, my dad was going to kick them out of the summer three-on-three league and then—"

Cody whirled around. "Your dad said that?"

"Well . . . no, he didn't say that. But they don't have to know he didn't say that. And I told them—"

"Wait . . . wait. You lied to them?" Cody pressed.

"Well, sort of. My dad didn't say those things, but it's a good kind of lie—even the part about him not letting them on the high school team next year."

"You told them that, too?"

"It was more like I hinted about that. Hey, but it helped, didn't it?"

Cody interlocked his fingers, put his hands behind his head, looked up at the scattered clouds in the sky, and sighed. "A good lie?"

"It's not bad to keep them out of trouble and—"

"And keep us from getting creamed!" Jeremiah finished.

"But you can't lie about it!" Cody protested.

"I do it all the time," Feather admitted. "What difference does it make? We haven't cheated them out of anything."

"But it's not right. What if they find out? Then they'll really be mad at us!"

"I figured it couldn't get any worse," Larry maintained. "Chill off, Clark. You're too uptight. I was doing you a favor, that's all. Is this the thanks I get?" Larry turned around and walked backwards up the gravel street. "Look, I think we should go over our game mistakes while they're all still fresh on our minds."

"Mistakes?" Jeremiah exploded. "We won!"

"Yes, but what can we do to play better ball next time we meet them?"

"Send *two* of them to California," Feather suggested.

Larry, Feather, and Jeremiah continued to talk about the game as Cody dropped back a few steps.

Lord, I wish Larry hadn't lied to them. I'm really glad to have J. J. not looking for a fight. But it could have been settled some other way. I know I prayed about it, but this can't be the answer. J. J. stills hates me and wants to beat me up. That hasn't changed. It just sort of postpones settling things up.

That's what lying always does—just postpones the consequences until things get worse.

Larry was just trying to help.

But I need Your help more than his.

"Come on, Clark, you're coming to my house, aren't you?"

Cody looked up. He had, without thinking, walked by Larry's driveway and headed home.

"Oh . . . yeah. I was just . . ."

"We know, we know," Feather speculated. "You were repenting for Larry's sins."

Larry stopped dribbling the ball. "My what?"

"Was I right?" she asked.

"Sort of. I guess. . . . Anyway, are we going to have practice at the ranch tomorrow?"

"Yeah, in the morning," Larry announced.

"Then we'll keep scouting for graves B, C, and D. Did you call your grandad about the note we found in that gun, Jeremiah?" Feather asked.

"He wasn't at home. I think he went to a pow-wow in Canada. But I don't figure he'd keep anything inside a gun except how much game he's shot this year."

Larry barged through the front door of his house, and Cody held it open for Jeremiah and Feather.

"A = antelope. Let's see. B = bear. C = coyotes, and . . . D, eh, deer!" Larry shouted. "All right! I broke the code! Am I good, or am I good?"

"What does the senseless slaughter of helpless wild animals for sport have to do with 'God is just'?" Feather lectured.

"Well," Jeremiah replied softly, "it's not for sport. It's food for Grandpa's table—and his Christmas present to all his kids."

"Larry might be right about one thing," Cody broke in. "There might be an easy explanation for all of this."

"But that's so boring. I figure the riddle is a clue that leads to a serial killer," Feather proclaimed.

"And we'll capture him and get to be on the national news. I can just see it now: 'Brave and good-looking gang of kids led by Jeremiah Yellowboy, pride of the Nez Perce Nation, risk their lives to capture vicious and ugly serial killer. Film at 11:00,'" Jeremiah recited.

Cody trailed the others downstairs to the Lewises' large family room. The west wall contained cupboards, a sink, and a refrigerator. The east wall housed a sixty-inch screen television. The carpet was thick, the colors light and cheerful, and the room smelled of fresh-cut flowers.

"Wow, this is a big room!" Feather squealed. "A person could make a house out of this one room."

"I spend a lot of time down here. Help yourself to a soda in the fridge. You want to see something cool? I've got a tape of the 1987 NCAA championship game. You've got to watch this. Indiana beat Syracuse by only one point! It's totally awesome on the big screen. Really!"

Jeremiah and Feather shook their heads.

"Nope," Cody replied firmly. "Larry, we aren't going to watch basketball. We aren't going to talk basketball. We aren't even going to think basketball—you got that?"

Larry looked dumbfounded. "You're joking, right?"

"Probably." Cody cracked a smile. "But don't go around making up any more stories to tell J. J. I'm not joking about that."

"You guys want to see my collection of Larry Bird basketball cards? I've got 102 different ones. It's probably the best LB collection in Idaho."

"Eh, sure." Cody shrugged.

"Great! Wait right here!" Larry sprinted out of the room and banged his way up the stairs.

Jeremiah stepped over to the big screen. "Boy, this is one great television. It would be cool to watch movies on it."

"Larry only owns one movie," Cody announced.

"Which one?" Feather questioned.

"*Hoosiers*," Cody laughed. "I'm kidding."

Larry bounced back into the room. "Did you guys say

you wanted to watch *Hoosiers?* I've got it in a letterbox laser disc edition. It is primo!"

"Show us the Larry Bird cards, Mr. Larry Bird Lewis," Cody insisted.

And he did.

The plan was to meet at the Clark house at 10:00 A.M. and ride their bikes to the ranch for team practice. Cody was ready half an hour early and dressed in his nylon shorts, sleeveless black T-shirt, basketball shoes—and straw cowboy hat.

The thirty-two-foot nylon rope circled his white wide-brimmed hat twice and then seemed to float out over the plastic steer head that was shoved into a bale of hay in his backyard. The rope settled down on the motionless prey as softly as the gentle breeze that blew out of the northwest.

Someday, Lord, I'd like to win a big silver buckle like Prescott and Reno and Denver. I know I'm not as good as they are. Maybe I never will be. But I'd only need to win one buckle. That would be enough really. My whole life I've had to try to catch up with them. They get to do everything first and second and third. Sometimes I think there's nothing new left for me. Like Reno giving me this rope after he didn't want it anymore and Prescott sending me the hat because he won it in Ogden, but it was too small for him.

Lord, I'm glad I've got great brothers, but it sure is tough being the pigtail. I can't rope like Prescott, get straight A's like Reno, or play basketball like Denver. I'm just me. I sure am glad You like me the way I am.

The rope once again circled the plastic head and pulled tight against its iron-post neck.

Sometime . . . somehow . . . I'm going to be the first Clark boy to do something!

"Nice throw, cowboy!"

Feather Trailer-Hobbs coasted up the narrow dirt alley on her red bike. "You going to wear that hat out to practice?"

"No. I just like wearing it when I rope. It keeps me from swinging my wrist too close to my head. You know what I mean?"

"Nope. But that's okay. Cody, is your mom home?"

"She works at the post office today. Did you need to talk to her?"

Feather balanced her bike and twisted her hair. "Yeah, but I can talk to her after practice."

"What about?" Cody asked.

"Oh, see—it's this thing about my mother."

"Did your mom have another spell?"

"No, no. Mom's just got it in her mind that she wants to go up and see my dad. He's up in the Dixie area protesting the Forest Service logging permits, and Mom wants to spend a week or so with him."

Cody coiled his rope and built another loop. "She probably misses him a lot."

"I guess. At least she needs a little money."

Cody roped the steer head again and went to retrieve his lasso. "Does he get paid for protesting?"

"Oh, yeah. And if Mom joins him, she'll get paid, too."

"So she makes money by going to see him?"

"Something like that. But here's the thing. I don't want to go. I want to stay here and play basketball. So I, you know . . . thought I'd ask your mom if I could stay with you guys a week or two."

"You what?" Cody gasped.

"You don't care, do you? Didn't you say you guys had a five-bedroom house? With only you and Denver at home, you must have a couple of spare rooms," she reasoned.

"Well, sure. When did you want to do this?"

"When does Denver have to go to basketball camp in Spokane?"

"That's after haying season. About the last week in July or so." Cody continued to rope the steer head.

"It would be sometime soon then. What do you think? Will she let me?"

"I, eh . . . I don't know. I mean, my brothers have never asked to let a girl stay at our house before."

"Well, then you'll get to be the first!"

Cody pushed his hat back on his head. *Lord, this is not the kind of first I had in mind. We can't have a girl in our house! We've never had girls stay at our house. Besides Mom. But moms don't count as girls.*

"Cody?" Feather wrinkled her nose and squinted her eyes. "It's all right with you if I stay at your house, isn't it? After all, you are my very best friend in the whole world."

I am? But we've only known each other two weeks.

"Cody?"

"Yeah, sure. It's, eh, all right with me. But that's something that my mom and dad have to decide."

"I knew you wouldn't mind. That's what I told my mom.

She said it would be all right if your mom agreed. She even said that if you ever needed a place, you could always come out and stay with us."

With Feather and her mother in a tepee? Meditating with the trees and burning candles and all that? Now that's scary.

"Hey, Lewis and Clark Squad," Larry shouted as he raced through the scattered pine trees on the vacant lots that separated his house from Cody's. "You won't believe this awesome practice schedule I developed last night. It will really surprise you."

"Somehow I doubt that," Feather muttered.

"No, really. Listen to this. We go out and shoot one game of 'bump'—just to limber up. Then we play two-on-two to twenty. Me and you, Feather, against Cody and Jeremiah. Then everyone gets to choose their favorite two drills—as long as they don't duplicate something we've already done. Then we play another two-on-two game, Me and Cody against Jeremiah and Feather. And that's it. What do you think?"

Cody looked at Feather. She nodded approval.

"I am surprised, Larry. That sounds pretty good to me, too."

"Hey, I do learn, you know. Where's Jeremiah?"

"Maybe he slept in. We can ride by his house and stir him up," Cody suggested.

"Are we going to look and see if there are any more gravestones with A or B or C or D on them over at Eureka Blaine's?" Feather asked.

"Why don't you guys look while I feed the horses. I've got to deworm them today."

"Do what?" Larry gasped.

"Just eject a tube of deworming paste into their mouths, that's all. It's no big deal—except for Two Doc Barb. He'll probably try to bite me."

"We'll go look for the markers," Larry agreed. "Can I use your bike?" he asked Cody.

"Yeah, let me put up my rope and hat."

"Did Cody tell you I'm going to stay with him a couple of weeks while my mom goes up to see my dad?" Feather blurted out.

"You're going to what?" Larry choked.

"Stay here at Denver's house," she announced.

Denver's house? That's why she wants to hang around here.

"Actually, Feather hasn't talked to my mother yet. So we don't know for sure—," Cody began.

"Your mom's so nice," Feather gushed. "I just know she'll let me do it."

"Yeah, Feather can help us with the haying," Cody tried to joke.

"Do I get paid?" she shot back.

"Eh, actually if any of you guys wanted to make some money, you could help me load hay."

"Really?" Larry asked. "Maybe we could save up some and buy ourselves some real uniforms."

Cody looked over and met Feather's eyes.

"Feather worked hard to make us the tie-dyed ones, and I think—"

"Larry's right," Feather interrupted. "The colors smear when you wash them. I think we should probably get new jerseys, too. But I don't like wearing tank tops."

"You could wear a T-shirt underneath," Cody suggested.

"That's cool. What color should we get?"

"Red and white!" Larry shouted. "Like Indiana."

Cody shook his head. "We'll talk about it out at the ranch. Come on, let's go get Townie."

Halt, Idaho, has almost 800 people, two paved streets, one fenced yard, and only half a dozen large homes. Most of the homes in the older part of town are company houses. Each is identical, built on a small lot by the big lumber mill that organized the town in the first place.

The mill is gone, but the mill houses remain. Most have been added onto over the years, making them look bulky and cumbersome. Many look run-down, but some are very well kept. The Yellowboy home was always one of the neatest of the mill houses. Fresh blue paint, white trim, white shutters, clean yard, well-weeded flower beds, and a screen door that never needed patching.

Cody left his bike with Larry and Feather at the street and hiked up to the Yellowboys' front door. He knocked several times.

"No one's home," he hollered back at Larry and Feather.

"There's always somebody there," Larry called back.

Cody knocked again. "Anyone home? Townie, are you sleeping?"

"They ain't home!"

The voice spoke from an open window of Alviso Spaulding's single-wide trailer house diagonally parked on a weedy, narrow lot next to Jeremiah's house.

"Do you know where they went, Mr. Spaulding?" Cody called to the unseen man.

"I reckon they all went to the hospital."

"Hospital?"

"That's where ambulances usually end up, ain't it?"

Cody ran up to the trailer. "Who went to the hospital?"

"The whole passel of 'em."

"But who was it that was sick or injured?"

"Don't know that. But it wasn't Jeremiah. He was herdin' those girls."

Three

●

*C*ody, where are you going?" Feather yelled as he pedaled toward D Street.

"To see Mr. Henry at the hardware."

"Why?" she shouted, trying to catch up. Larry, his basketball tucked under his left arm, pedaled a distant third.

"Mr. Henry's an Emergency Medical Technician. He'll
know why they had to call an ambulance."

The Halt Hardware & Dry Goods hadn't changed much
since it was built in 1923—a two-story brick building with
apartments, then a dance floor, and finally inventory storage up above. A worn-wooden-floored store crammed with
everything from harnesses for draft horses, to animal
traps and snowshoes, to video games and designer toilet
fixtures—all on the lower floor.

The family still operated the business with several gen-
erations of Henrys working alongside each other. The only
nonfamily employee, Delbert O'Brian, began working at
Henry's when he returned from the war in 1945.

But Cody wasn't looking for just any old Henry. He

needed to find Tank Henry, and Tank spent most of his time fixing folks' plumbing, wiring, and roofs. In between house calls, Tank was the captain of the volunteer fire department and head of the EMT team.

Lord Jesus, You've got to help Townie and his family. I don't know what it is, but it must be serious. Please, Lord, keep it from being something too serious.

Cody dropped his bicycle on the wooden sidewalk in front of the hardware. He leaped the two front steps and crashed through the swinging screen doors.

"Hi, Cody! What can I get you?"

"Mrs. Henry, have you seen Mr. Henry?"

"Junior or senior?"

"Eh, junior."

"Tank just went out to Pilphers' to fix a washing machine. Can I help you?"

Feather and Larry scurried up behind him.

"I heard there was an ambulance call at Yellowboys' this morning. I was wondering what happened. I . . . eh, we were worried about Jeremiah."

"Tank said it was Carmen."

"Townie's mother? What happened?"

"Now that I couldn't tell you, except that Tank figured it might be a heart attack. That woman works too hard, if you ask me. Runnin' that tribal cafe, raisin' them kids, and all that church work."

"Heart attack? But she's not that old," Cody gulped.

"Is she dead?" Larry asked.

"I don't think so. Sorry, kids, I really don't know anything else."

"Thanks, Mrs. Henry."

"Cody, tell your daddy that box of swather bolts came in."

"Yes, ma'am."

Cody led them back out to the boardwalk. "I don't understand why that has to happen," he mumbled. "Mrs. Yellowboy is the nicest lady in town."

"Maybe it's not all that serious," Feather tried to console him. "Like when my mom has one of her bad spells. She gets over them quick."

"But they don't send someone in the ambulance to a hospital forty miles away if it's not serious, do they?" Cody argued.

"Boy, this really changes our practice schedule." Larry dribbled the ball next to his bike.

"Are you more worried about basketball practice?" Feather snarled, like a teacher about to write a detention notice.

"Oh, no . . . Maybe we should wait and practice this afternoon."

Feather stole Larry's ball and faked throwing it down the street.

"No . . . wait! Maybe tomorrow? We could cancel today's practice entirely." Larry choked out each word.

"Well, what are we going to do?" Feather asked Cody as she bounced Larry's ball back to him.

"I don't know. . . . I've got to feed Mr. Blaine's horses. You guys want to ride out there with me?"

"We could investigate that tombstone. You said there might be other ones," Feather suggested.

"And then we could . . . you know," Larry added, "if we

felt like it . . . shoot a few buckets just to get our minds off worrying about Jeremiah."

Cody nodded, climbed on his bike, and pedaled toward First Street.

Lord, sometimes it's like everything's a game. I feed the horses, play basketball, rope a little, eat supper, read a book, watch TV, go to bed, and then start all over again. Nothing dangerous. Nothing threatening. Nothing serious.

Then something like this happens. This is serious. This is real. This is important. This isn't fun.

Mrs. Henry's right. Jeremiah's mom works real hard. And You said the righteous would be rewarded. Well, it seems to me it's her time for a reward or two.

They rode out County Line Road without speaking. Even after turning off on the gravel side road, they traveled single file—Cody first, then Feather. Larry trailed behind toting his basketball. They turned down Eureka Blaine's driveway and parked their bikes in the shade of the big cottonwood tree in the backyard.

"Are you going to do that . . . deworm thing with the horses?" Larry asked.

"Yeah."

"Well, if you don't mind, I'll do something else."

"Why don't you go find that gravestone?" Cody suggested. "Feather, do you want to go with Larry?"

"I'll help you with the horses," she replied in a soft voice.

Cody was startled to see her eyes red and her cheeks tear-streaked. They walked to the old barn while Larry climbed the corral fence and sprinted off toward the woods.

"Have you been crying?" Cody asked.

"Sort of."

Cody opened the white-smudged cabinet and pulled out six syringes of Zimecterin paste. "What about?"

"I was just thinking of Jeremiah's mom. What if it were my mom? My mom does some crazy things. And you saw her last week, what she's like when she has one of her bad spells. But they're not all that serious. I'm used to those things. But what if my own mother died, Cody? That's really, really scary. My mom's about all I have. Dad doesn't like hanging around much, and I don't even know any other relatives."

Cody ambled toward the corral with the mares. "Everybody has relatives."

"Yeah, but see, my mom and dad said their families were too tied to the corporate destruction of America, and they would never speak to any of them again." She plucked one of the syringes out of Cody's hands. "What does this stuff do?" she asked as she examined the Zimecterin.

"It says on the label."

"It controls 'large and small strongyles, pinworms, ascarids, hair worms, stomach worms, neck threadworms, lungworms, intestinal threadworms and bots.' Oh, yuuck!" She shoved the syringe back into Cody's hand.

"Gross, huh? I just tell the horses it's candy."

"You do? You talk to the horses?"

"Sure. Your mom talks to the trees, doesn't she?"

"Well, yeah . . . but that's different. My mom's sort of weird. Do the horses ever talk back?"

"They don't say much," Cody admitted, "but I can tell they're listening."

"I wonder what that stuff tastes like?"

Cody chuckled. "Now there's a mystery I have no intention of solving. Watch Bulah and Marti. They love this stuff."

Both mares trotted to the coral fence. Cody stood on the bottom rail and leaned forward.

"Snack time, girls," he called. "One at a time. Now get back there, Marti. You wait your turn. . . . That's it. You know Bulah will pitch a fit if you crowd in front of her." Cody turned to Feather. "And she will, too. There's only two of them, but Bulah thinks she's in charge."

The horses eagerly sucked on the syringe as Cody pushed the plunger in, forcing the paste onto their tongues. They stepped away smacking their lips as if they had peanut butter stuck to the roofs of their mouths.

"That's all there is to it? I thought you had to give them a shot or something," Feather quizzed.

"Nope. I don't have to give shots until the fall."

"Really? You *do* give them shots?"

"It's no big deal." He shrugged, moving toward another corral.

"It is to me!" Feather exclaimed. "I've never had a shot in my life."

"Really?"

"My mother doesn't believe in them."

Feather watched quietly as Cody dewormed the two geldings. They walked to the final corral where Sonny Boy waited for them at the gate.

"Cody, do you ever think about your mom dying?" Feather blurted out.

"Not much. It's one of those things I just don't want to think about."

"It could happen though. People do die. I think about dying all the time."

Cody glanced over at Feather. Her bangs hung down to her eyes. Her long, thin brown hair flopped about her shoulders. She looked very much alive. "Why do you think about dying?"

"I guess because it scares me so much. . . . Does it scare you, Cody?"

"Oh, a little, I guess. But I just figure all of that is up to the Lord. He'll take care of me."

He scooped out a handful of oats from a big plastic garbage can that had been converted to a grain storage bin.

"I wish I had met you when we were young, Cody Clark."

"We *are* young. We're barely thirteen."

"Well, I would have liked to learn about your God when I was little and didn't have these other ideas crammed into my head."

"Jesus said we all have to come to Him like a little child, no matter what our age."

"Are you preaching at me, Cody Wayne Clark?"

"Probably . . . eh, do you want to do me a really, really big, fat favor?" Cody asked.

"Sure, what?"

"I need you to twitch Two Doc Barb when he comes over to eat these oats out of my hand."

"Twitch him?"

"Yeah, grab his left ear and twist it real hard. Just hold on while I get him to take the paste."

"Twist his ear? You mean, like hurt him?"

"Just a little discomfort."

"Why do you want me to treat him inhumanely?"

"Well, first he's a horse—not a human, so how can you be inhumane to him? But also he needs this medicine so all those yucky worms you read about won't make him sick."

"How does twisting his ear help?"

"Horses usually only think about one thing at a time. If you can get him thinking about his ear, he'll forget about what I'm doing to his mouth."

"That really works?"

"Most times."

"What if he forgets about his ear and remembers what you're doing?"

"He'll probably bite me—and you."

"Oh, great!"

"Don't worry, I'll keep his head turned this way. Trust me."

"Okay, I'll try it, but this had better work, Cody Clark!"

I was thinking the exact same thing!

The golden chestnut stallion, with the white star and stripe on his nose and white half stocking on his left front leg, grazed his way closer to them.

"As soon as he goes for the oats in my hand, grab his ear and twist. Don't let go!"

Two Doc cautiously approached the pair perched on the corral fence and whinnied. Cody reached his right oat-filled hand over the rail. In his left hand, held behind his back, was the deworming syringe.

"Come on, boy . . . time for treats. Come on, that-a-boy. . . . This is Feather. She's really nice, and she won't hurt you . . . much. Here he comes. Are you ready, Feather girl?"

"I'm a little scared."

"Nothing to it. Just twist the ear and hang on."

"Are you sure this works?"

"Actually I've never tried it with Two Doc."

"Oh, great!"

"Now, Feather girl!" he ordered as the horse began to gobble the oats.

The second Two Doc felt his ear being twisted, he stopped chewing the oats and stared straight at Feather. He didn't kick. He didn't bite. He didn't flinch. He didn't move a muscle.

Cody immediately shoved the tube into the horse's mouth and emptied its contents.

"Now what?" Feather asked.

"Pull your hand back fast, and I'll try to get him to finish eating his oats."

Feather yanked her hand back, and Two Doc snapped his teeth at her.

"He tried to bite me!" she hollered.

"He's just a little ticked off. Here, boy . . . eat your oats!"

Suddenly Two Doc Barb reared on his hind legs, kicked his front hooves over Cody's and Feather's heads, and spun around, running to the lower end of the pasture.

"A little ticked off?" Feather gasped.

"At least he didn't bust a rail trying to get at us. Come on, help me toss them all a few flakes of hay. Then we'll go find Larry."

When they arrived at the clearing, Larry Lewis was hunched behind the concrete marker, digging in the dirt with a stick.

"What are you doing?" Cody called out.

Lewis jumped straight up and then relaxed when he saw it was Cody and Feather. "Hi, guys. I'm conducting a little investigation here."

"It looks like you're digging up someone's grave," Feather fussed.

"Ah hah! Feather, our sweet prairie princess, that's where you are mistaken!"

Sweet prairie princess? Cody silently mouthed at her. Feather held her hands around her throat and faked a gag.

"Come here and look. Just look," Larry urged.

They hiked around the cactus patch in front of the marker to join Larry and his basketball behind the slab of concrete.

He grasped the edge of the marker. "Now what do you see?"

"The back of a headstone?" Feather suggested.

"Let me present the facts," Larry lectured. "There are no other stones around here, and this clearing is not big enough to be a regular graveyard—even years ago, correct?"

Cody looked around and then nodded his head.

"Second, most grave markers are made out of stone—are they not?"

"Either that or little brass plaques," Cody agreed.

"Right. And this is certainly not a brass plaque, and it's concrete—not stone. Am I correct?"

"Continue, Detective Lewis."

"Inspector Lewis," Larry corrected.

"Chief Inspector Lewis," Feather teased.

"Now . . . look down here below the dirt level. What do you see?"

"Dirty concrete?" Feather offered.

"Dirty, broken-edged concrete."

"Like this was a piece of a concrete wall or something," Cody suggested.

"Bingo! My friends, what if this isn't a gravestone? What if it's just an old piece of a concrete wall that's been dumped in the ravine to keep it from being an eyesore some other place?"

"Like that old part of a car Jeremiah found down here last week!" Feather said, her excitement building.

Cody scratched the back of his brown bushy hair and rubbed his arms. In the shade of the brush-lined ravine, the air felt a little cool. "I think Larry's right about the concrete. This only looks like a marker. And the words 'God is just' are painted on, not chiseled."

He stood silent for a moment. "But how did it just happen to land with the writing facing the correct way, and how did the brush clear itself out, and why did two dozen prickly pear cactus plants just happen to spring up in front of it?"

Larry bent down and retied his shoe. Then he rubbed

the back of his hand on his nose, leaving a dirt smear. "Yeah. I was wondering that too. It's sort of like this was an old wall off of something, and someone decided to use it for a grave marker."

"Or some kind of marker. Maybe it's not a grave," Feather conjectured. "Maybe something important is buried here. Like money or jewels . . . something like that."

Cody stooped down and ran his fingers along the jagged edge of broken concrete. "I keep wondering what this has to do with the note we found in Jeremiah's grandfather's gun."

"I got it! I got it!" Feather shouted. "Someone used the gun to hold up banks—four of them. One in a town that started with an A. Another with a B and so on. And they buried all the money out here by this marker that was in the ravine anyway. They planted the cactus so that people would think it's an old grave and stay away from it. But they intended to come back at a later date and dig up their loot after things cooled down. But they got in a car wreck and died, so the money's been buried here all these years. What do you think?"

"You ought to be a writer." Cody grinned.

"It's really that good, huh?"

"It's really novel," Larry teased.

"Very funny. Why don't you go get a shovel, and I'll prove it to you."

"Are you serious?" Cody asked. "What if someone is buried here? What if we dig down and find a skeleton?"

Larry's face turned snow-white as he gasped for air. "I'm getting dizzy!"

"Sit down and put your head between your knees," Feather instructed. "I say, it could have happened just like I said."

"Are you saying that Jeremiah's grandfather was a bank robber, or is it his great-grandfather?" Cody quizzed.

"Oh, well, I never thought—I mean . . ."

"Besides, who would rob a bank with a big rifle like that. Wouldn't you use a handgun? A rifle is too bulky and awkward."

"Well, what's your explanation?" Feather asked.

"I don't have one, but I do think it would be interesting to know if anything is buried under the cactus."

"You want me to go to your barn and find a shovel?" Feather offered.

"I don't think we can dig on Eureka's property without his permission."

"But he'll be gone for weeks," Feather said. "You're in charge of looking after the place in the meantime. All you have to do is give yourself permission to dig, right?"

"Ugh. I think . . . I'd better think it over before we do that."

"Oh, you mean that talk-to-God thing you do?" she asked.

"Yeah. It just seems a little weird to dig up someone's cactus patch. What if it was a grave of one of Eureka's family? That wouldn't be right."

Feather sighed. "I hate it when you're right, Cody Clark!"

Larry stood up. Color had come back to his face. "I've got an idea." He beamed.

"What's that?"

"How about a little two-on-one over at the barn. I'll take you both on, and we'll play to twenty. Then we can switch off after I cream you."

"This could be real ugly," Feather retorted and wrinkled her nose. "No crying, Larry, when you get humiliated."

"Cry? Me? I've got six plays that will blow you away!" Larry bragged as they climbed out of the ravine.

"Plays? How can you have a play? There's only one of you on the team," Cody challenged.

"In fact, this is liable to be too easy," Larry boasted. "I wish Jeremiah was here. Then I could play three-on-one. It would be more fair."

"Yeah," Cody sighed, "I wish Townie was here, too."

Four

❖

*T*hat was the luckiest shot in the history of barn basketball!" Larry wailed as they pedaled their bikes back to town.

"We call that play Barn Bounce #37," Feather teased.

"Oh, sure, now you're going to tell me it was all planned. You didn't even hit the backboard. It bounced off the side of the barn. It would have been an air ball in the bleachers any other place!"

"You got beat, Lewis," Feather declared. "Just admit you couldn't take us."

"I don't even think that shot was legal!" Larry huffed, trying to keep up with the longer legs of Cody and Feather.

"You're the one who said we could count barn shots," Cody reminded him.

"Yeah, but I didn't count on you abusing it like that. It's a wonder you didn't throw the ball up into the loft."

"Relax, L. B., we barely beat you. I thought you were playing great," Cody praised him.

"You really think so?"

"Yep."

Larry stood straight up on the pedals and coasted. "I was shooting the lights out, wasn't I?"

"On fire," Cody declared. "You two beat me by ten points."

When they reached the edge of town, Cody turned down Joseph Avenue.

"Where are you going?" Larry called out.

"I'm going to check with my mom at the post office," Cody hollered. "Maybe she knows something about Townie's mother by now."

"I'm coming with you," Feather called back. "I want to talk to your mom myself."

"Well, I'm going home to work on some more one-on-two plays. I really think I can take you next time." Larry cruised straight up First Street.

Cody coasted to allow Feather to catch up. *How can a one-man team have plays? Get the ball—make a basket. What else is there? Lord, was Larry just born like that, or is that what happens when you grow up in a coach's family? I don't think I've ever known anyone with such a one-track mind.*

Main Street of Halt, Idaho, has seen its better days. In the 1920s the town was a lumber mill boom town. Retail businesses lined six whole blocks on both sides. Banks, theaters, shops, and saloons fought for space. And in the evenings, the citizens just plain fought.

Those days are long gone. Now most of the old buildings have burned down, been torn down, or sit empty, waiting to fall down. Most businesses are now scattered along the paved Highway 95 bypass on the south edge of town. The hardware store and post office are still downtown along with half a dozen other businesses in various stages of failure.

The post office is one of the newer buildings, a post-World War II brick one-story building erected in 1951 on the site of the famous Halt Hotel. It was said that after an elk-hunting expedition, former President Theodore Roosevelt and the legendary Arizona lawman, Stuart Brannon, stayed at the Halt Hotel. Cody once looked it up in a biography of Roosevelt and didn't find Halt mentioned. But everyone at the senior citizens' weekly luncheon swore that it's true. Some, even though not old enough, claimed they had met both men personally.

Cody figured that Halt liked to hold on to its heritage—whether it be fact or fiction.

They parked the bikes by the worn and initial-carved wooden bench in front of the post office and traipsed in through the aluminum-framed glass door that stood propped open with a rock the size of a shot put. "I should have checked with Mom earlier. When she works at the post office, she hears everything about everyone."

"This is bigger than I thought," Feather observed as she stood and stared at row after row of small brass boxes with tiny windows, numbers, and key slots.

Cody tapped on one. "There's ours—157. Don't you guys have a box? Oh, I guess you're on the rural route."

"Actually . . ." Feather looked down at her red-dust-covered black canvas basketball shoes. "We don't get any mail. I've never gotten a letter or a card mailed to me in my whole life. Not that I care a twit about it, mind you," she quickly added. "My folks don't believe in using the mail."

"They don't—"

"Don't say anything, Cody, please!"

"Hey, that's cool. They sure have a lot of things they do and don't believe in. Let's go see Mom."

Lord, it's like her parents are from another planet. They seem to be concerned with just about everything except what's important. What's wrong with getting mail? I guess You'll have to help me be more tolerant of other people who are different—really different.

"Hi, Mom!" he blurted out, sounding louder than he intended.

Although she was only twenty-one on her wedding day, Cody's mom had looked thirty years old when she married Hank Clark. That was twenty-five years ago, and she still looked thirty. Margaret Clark was attractive, knowledgeable, and gave a sense of seasoned control. She was equally at home delivering a calf, a colt, a lecture, or the mail. She looked relaxed in Wranglers and boots—or in a lacy dress. Cody figured she was about the prettiest woman in town. Not counting Mrs. Franklin, who used to be a model and always wore that big blonde wig and all that makeup.

"Well, hi, you two! Feather, your hair sure looks cute braided down the sides like that."

"Thanks, Mrs. Clark. I'm glad someone noticed! Eh, when Cody's done, I need to talk to you."

Cody stared at Feather.

Her hair is different? Doesn't she always do that?

"Cody Wayne, did Jeremiah find you?" Mrs. Clark queried as he walked up to the counter.

"No, ma'am. I was going to ask you about his mother. I heard she was taken off in an ambulance."

"Yes. It was just exhaustion, not her heart, bless her soul. She called to talk to me a little while ago."

"She's home already?" Cody quizzed.

"No, they want to observe her overnight at the hospital. But she's going to need to take a vacation and go rest up at her sister's in Yakima."

"To Yakima? Right away?" Cody pressed.

"The girls are going with her. Two Ponies and Sweetwater are going out on a fire-fighting crew."

"How about Townie? We need him on our team. How many games is he going to miss?"

"That's exactly what he said. So I told Carmen that Jeremiah could stay with us for the next two weeks."

"Really? All right!" He turned to Feather. "Is that cool or what?"

Feather's eyes narrowed. He felt her tense up. She turned to the door.

"Did you want to talk to me, Feather?" Cody's mom called out.

"I'll talk to you later, Mrs. Clark. There's no hurry . . . now." She walked back out to the room with all the post office boxes.

"Cody, Jeremiah's looking for you. He'll be bringing some gear over. Let him have Reno's room. If he doesn't find you in town, he'll be riding out to the ranch looking for you."

"We didn't see him."

"Perhaps he's at his place. I'll be home about 4:30. Don't mess up the house too much."

"Yes, ma'am."

Cody sprinted out. Feather stood staring at old photographs of Halt that lined one wall of the post office.

"Isn't that great? Townie's mom is going to be all right. That's an answer to prayer!"

"I noticed you were pretty excited when you found out Jeremiah's going to stay with you a couple of weeks."

"Yeah, it will be so awesome. We can play video games and go hunting and . . ." Feather's eyes teared up. "What's wrong?"

"You didn't act that way when I said I wanted to stay at your house."

"But you're a girl. It's different. And I . . . I don't know anything about girls." Cody shrugged.

"That's for sure." She sniffed.

"Come on, let's go find Townie."

Feather didn't move. "These photographs are really something. It's hard to imagine Halt once looked like this. Look at this. They had horse-drawn street cars."

"And a jail. Those two up there are pictures of the old jail. Sort of a before and after."

Feather stood on tiptoes and squinted. "Before and after what?"

"The bomb. You've heard about the big bomb blast, haven't you?"

"Bomb? There was a bomb in Halt?"

"It's in all the Idaho history books. Remember when you were in the fourth grade and studied Idaho history?"

"In the fourth grade I studied the Environmental Impact of Nineteenth-Century Expansionist Colonial Culture on Native American Tribes in the Pacific Northwest."

"You've got to be kidding," Cody choked. "What's all of that mean?"

"I'm home-schooled, remember? That was the title of my dad's doctoral dissertation."

"Your dad has a doctorate?"

"So what? So does my mom."

"She does? What in?"

"In postmodern European existentialism."

"What in the world is that?"

"I'm not sure." Feather shrugged. "But don't ever ask her to explain it."

"Why? What will happen?"

"She'll explain it." Feather glanced back up at the wall. "So tell me about the jail and the bomb."

"Well, there's the picture up there—see the jail? It was just a concrete and iron-bar job, I guess. You can see it on the left. Some Chicago gangster wanted for murder—I forget his name—was hiding out in the canyons around here. He got arrested by the FBI and put into jail at Halt until they could extradite him. I guess some of his buddies showed up to help him escape. Anyway, they tried to blow open the jail, but they used so much explosives that it was literally a bomb. It collapsed the whole building. Look at that other picture. See what I mean?"

Feather shielded her eyes from the sunlight coming through the window and continued to stare at the photo near the ceiling.

"There was nothing left but a pile of rubble. They never rebuilt the jail. They just started using the county one after that."

Feather turned to Cody. "What about the guy in jail? Did he escape?"

"No, he was killed when the roof crashed in on him."

"Wow, some friends, huh?" Feather continued to look at the faded black-and-white photograph. "Cody, what does it say on that old jail?"

"Where?"

"See, there's something written on that piece of jail wall."

"I don't know . . . I can't read it. It probably just says keep off or something like that. My grandma was teaching school when the bomb went off, and she said it felt like an earthquake."

Feather stretched on her tiptoes again. "Cody, lift me up so I can read it."

He sensed his face blush red. "Are you kidding?"

"You can lift me up, can't you?"

"But . . . I . . . it's not . . ." Cody felt beads of sweat form on his forehead and on the palms of his hands.

"Oh, for pete's sake, Cody. Sometimes boys can act so stupid! Come here, I'll lift you up, and you read the sign!"

"No, no, I'll lift."

"Well?" she scoffed. Her eyes flashed above her folded arms.

The sweat rolled off his face. He glanced around. No one else was in the lobby. "Eh . . . how do I lift you up?" Each word felt like a golf ball stuck in his throat.

Feather shook her head in disgust. "Bend down, grab me around the knees, and lift me straight up!"

"Really?" Cody's eyes widened. He felt short of breath.

Feather sighed and rolled her eyes. "We're not getting married, Cody Wayne Clark! You're just lifting me up to read that sign. You're acting like some nerd who's never touched a girl before. You have touched a girl, haven't you?"

"Oh . . . sure," he stammered and swallowed hard. *But not since that kiss from Honey Del Mateo in the first grade.*

Cody bent down, stared for a moment at her bony knees, and wrapped his arms around them as if they were a sack of rolled oats. Feather put her hands on his shoulders for balance. When the skin on his bare arms touched her, he wished he'd worn a long-sleeved shirt instead of the sleeveless T-shirt. But he was surprised at how light Feather was. *She's a whole lot lighter than a sack of feed!* Her legs felt thin and smooth.

"Cody! That's it!" She shouted so abruptly he almost dropped her. "Move me closer to the wall."

He staggered a bit but managed to move right up against the wall without smashing her into any of the photos. "What do you see?"

"Right there on that piece of concrete among the ruins of the old jail. It says, 'God is just'!"

Cody scrunched his face around and tried to look up at her. "'God is just'? You mean just like the saying in the gun and on that marker out at Eureka's?"

"This *is* the marker! What we found out there was a piece of the old jail."

"No kidding? It really says that?"

"I'm sure it's the same piece. What do you think it means, Cody?"

"I have no idea in the world. But it sure brings up more questions than it answers. We still don't know why that saying is on the paper in the gun or why it's out at Eureka's. And now we don't know why someone painted it on the old jail in the first place or what that riddle means."

"Well, is that a new dance?" A woman's voice boomed through the post office door.

Cody's heart sank. Mrs. Keuther had just barged in for her mail.

"No, ma'am . . . I, eh . . . we're just, eh . . . ," Cody stammered.

"Cody just lifted me up to look at the photographs," Feather explained smoothly.

"Well, it certainly looks like . . . eh, fun." Mrs. Keuther nodded. "Cody Clark, I don't believe I know this young lady. Introduce me to your little friend."

"I'm not his 'little' friend. I'm as tall as he is, maybe taller. My name is Feather Trailer-Hobbs."

"Well, there you have it. Now if you two could waltz over this way, I'll be able to get to my box."

"Oh, yeah!" Cody staggered toward the door, still carrying Feather.

"You can put me down now!" she instructed.

Put her down? Oh, man, I hope no one else saw us!

Cody released his grip, and Feather dropped straight down, landing on her feet with a loud slap of basketball shoes on the concrete floor. He scurried out the door to the bicycles without looking back.

"I always wondered what it felt like when a boy dropped you. But I never took it literally before," she teased.

"I'm sorry, Feather. I didn't mean to . . . I mean, I was starting to feel kind of flustered."

Feather laced her fingers together and pushed her palms outward. "That's an understatement."

Cody steered his bike toward the west side of town. Feather stood on the pedals and pumped hard to keep up. Her very long braids blew behind her like pennants.

"Where are you going?" she called out.

"To find Townie."

"I've got to go home and help my mom," she hollered.

"I'll see you in the morning for practice," Cody called back.

"Yeah. But don't you guys go out there to that marker until in the morning! You promise?"

"I promise."

"Okay. I'll see you tomorrow. And thanks, Cody."

"For what?"

"For lifting me up to see the pictures. Some boys wouldn't have done that."

"You're welcome."

And some boys won't do it again! Cody felt the sweat begin to bead on his forehead again.

Feather headed home out the old stage road, and Cody turned up the steep gravel drive that led to his and Larry's houses. Even though the rest of the property around them was subdivided into city lots, it remained pine-covered and undeveloped.

Jeremiah Yellowboy sat on the concrete steps of Cody's front porch. His bicycle leaned against a post, and a duffel bag lay at his side.

"Townie, how's your mom?" Cody called as he sailed into the yard.

Jeremiah rubbed his eyes with the back of his right hand. "She's going to be all right. The doctor said it was stress more than anything."

"It sure sounded scary. . . . Were you scared?" Cody flopped his bike on the grass and scooted over toward Jeremiah.

"Yeah. Scared. Confused. I didn't know what to do. It didn't seem like I could do anything for her, so I just rounded up the girls and kept them occupied. I thought she was dying, Cody!"

Lord, I wish I could say something to make Townie feel better. But if I don't watch out, I'm going to start bawling.

"Hey, Mom said you're going to stay with us a couple of weeks. Is that cool or what?"

"I'll miss my mother," Jeremiah responded, his voice soft and low.

"Oh, man, Townie, if I sit around here any longer, I'll start crying like some girl!"

"Better not let Feather hear you say that."

"Yeah, come on in. Mom said you can use Reno's room."

Both boys pushed their way into the tri-level, two-tone brown house. Jeremiah followed Cody down the stairs to the bedroom at the end of the hall.

"This is bodacious," Jeremiah called, looking around the room plastered with rodeo photographs, trophies, ribbons, and buckles.

"No, that is Bodacious over there—the big white Sammy Andrews bull. His name is Bodacious, but they retired him. He kept busting up cowboys. Reno rode him for two seconds one time. He said it was two seconds too long. That's when Reno gave up bull-riding and decided to stick with timed events."

"A room all to myself. I could get used to this."

"Well, don't get too used to it. Feather wants to stay over here when her mom goes up to see her dad."

"She does? A girl at your house? Don't do it, Cody. I've got four sisters, and they try to control everything I do."

"Well, she's got to talk to my mom yet."

Jeremiah flopped on his back on Reno's bed and spread his arms and legs wide. "Imagine going to sleep in a big, ol' room in a big, ol' bed like this. It must make a person feel guilty."

Not until you brought the subject up.

"Townie, listen. Have I got some news to tell you about that marker out at Eureka's!"

"Did you find some more of them out there?"

"No, but this is really going to knock your socks off. You want the long version or the short version?"

"I've got two weeks." Jeremiah finally grinned through his straight, white teeth. "Give me the long version. Tell me everything."

Cody did.

Five

Donnie Barnes took the pass from his brother and
turned to shoot the three-pointer from the top of the key.
Larry Lewis flew into the air and blocked the shot so hard
that the ball came right back at Donnie. It bounced off the
top of his head and into the hands of Jeremiah Yellowboy.

Donnie couldn't keep from giggling.

Jeremiah's pass went through the legs of Ronnie
Barnes. When he bent over to stop the ball, he fell flat on
the floor.

And started chuckling.

By then Dan Brinkoff, standing under the basket, was
laughing so hard the net shook as he stared up at the gym
ceiling lights.

Cody made the easy lay-in, and the entire Lewis and
Clark Squad joined in the laughter.

"Hey, I meant to do that!" Donnie howled. "Was that
an illegal defense?"

"Illegal?" Ronnie roared. "How about my dive? A guy

could win the gold with a dive like that. I got four 10s and 9.5 from the Russian judge!"

Tears streamed down Dan's cheeks. He rested his hand on his knees.

"It's your ball." Cody bounced the basketball out to Donnie.

"Hey, let's try that play again!" Donnie roared. "We call that our Three Stooges Three Play. The only thing that would have been funnier is if Ronnie's shorts had ripped!"

Cody felt good.

The High Plains Pioneers were not the best team in the Three-on-Three Summer Youth League.

But they were the most fun.

The Barnes twins were identical—in basketball, in school, in looks, and in constant laughter. They laughed when they shot, laughed when they missed, and laughed when the other team made one. They laughed coming into the gym, and they laughed when they left. Cody couldn't tell Ronnie from Donnie. Both shot three-pointers, played good defense, and passed fairly well, but neither could jump or drive or dribble worth spit.

But it didn't bother them—or Big Dan Brinkoff.

There was no "three seconds in the key" rule for summer three-on-three, and Big Dan parked under the front rim of the basket for the whole night. He didn't run. He didn't jump. He didn't dribble.

But he did get rebounds, make an occasional lay-in— and laughed. He could outlaugh anyone in school. When Dan laughed, the entire gym seemed to shake with joy. The sight that made Big Dan laugh most was the Barnes twins. Everything they did became a source of hysteria for him.

The Lewis and Clark Squad won the game twenty to twelve. It was never close. In fact, there was so much laughing that the Squad abandoned Larry's well-thought-out game plan and just fired up some shots when they were open.

Which was often.

But the Pioneers took it in cheerful stride. In fact, their cheerful stride headed out of the gym and down Joseph Avenue, straight for a milkshake at the Treat and Eat drive-in immediately after the game.

"All right!" Larry beamed as he, Cody, and Jeremiah clustered at the drinking fountain at the front of the gym. "We're on a roll. A three-game winning streak. Is our team great or what? Watch out, play-offs, we're on our way!"

"Of course, we do have thirty more games before we reach the end of the season," Cody reminded him.

"And I'm not sure beating the Pioneers is a great victory. They haven't won a game this season," Jeremiah pointed out.

"Well, there's thirty more golden opportunities to demonstrate our abundance of skill, discipline, and good coaching."

Jeremiah whistled. "Are you talking about our team?"

"And humility. He forgot to mention how humble we are," Cody added.

"Sometimes it's tough to be humble when you're this good," Larry replied. He wasn't even grinning.

Cody noticed that Jeremiah was shaking his head. *Lord, I think Larry sincerely means it.*

"I wish Feather had been here," Cody remarked. "She would have had a lot of fun tonight. She didn't mention to me anything about missing a game. Do you suppose something's wrong with her mom again?"

"You going to ride your bike out and check on her?" Jeremiah asked.

"I've been thinking about it. You don't have to go if you don't want to."

"I need to wait for that phone call from my mother," Jeremiah reported.

"How about you, Larry? Something must have been pretty serious for her to miss a game and not even let us know. You want to ride a bike out to Feather's with me?"

"Feather? Oh . . . no, you go on. It did seem strange for her not to be here, didn't it? Listen, I'm going to stay and watch the Pine Creek Porcupines play the Snake River Rams."

"Why?" Cody asked.

"To scout both teams. We play them next week, so I'll have to come up with game plans."

"Scout them out? More game plans?" Jeremiah laughed. It was the kind of a laugh you have when you read a headline from the tabloids near the checkout stand at the supermarket.

Larry seemed to miss the humor. "I'll print up scouting reports for each of us by practice tomorrow."

"Hey, I don't believe it! There's my grandad!" Jeremiah hollered.

Cody glanced into the stands to see a dark-skinned older man with a long gray ponytail drooping out the back of a Seattle Mariners baseball cap. His long-sleeved turquoise shirt was buttoned at the neck and looked starched and freshly ironed. The elderly man wore old jeans and cowboy boots, one of which had been repaired by wrapping wide gray duct tape around it. The wrinkles in his face seemed older and more permanent than the Rocky Mountains themselves. His eyes were dark brown and had a kind tint, but they were focused solely on Jeremiah.

"Grandpa, how'd you like the game? Did you see me make those three-pointers from the corner?"

Cody walked with Jeremiah up into the stands at the far end of the gym.

"You release the ball much too slowly. That's why the twin was able to block you—twice." The old man stepped gingerly down off the bleachers and then motioned with his hands. "You catch the ball with your shoulders squared to the basket, then swing it up into position, and shoot. If you can count to three before you release it, it's too slow."

Jeremiah's smile was as wide as his face. The old man stepped forward and gave him a big hug. "My grandfather is a good coach."

"Young Mr. Clark, it is good to see you again."

"Yes, sir, Mr. Yellowboy. How has your health been? I heard you were too sick to come hunting."

"Jeremiah worries too much. The day I can no longer hunt I will hike out into the forest and die. I am much better now. And how is your grandfather?"

"He's sort of slow after that heart surgery, but they say by next fall he should be fine."

"That's good! Tell him I will come down in October, and we'll hunt elk."

"Yes, sir, I'll tell him."

"What are you doing here, Grandpa?" Jeremiah asked. "I didn't know you were coming. Last I heard, you were in Canada at a pow-wow."

"My baby girl needed me. I came down to drive your mother to your Aunt Lucy's. But she needed more things from the house, so I drove up to get you to help me find the things on this list." He unbuttoned the flap on his shirt pocket and carefully opened a neatly folded yellow note. "After we're through, perhaps I will buy you a buffalo burger at the tribal cafe . . . providing Mrs. Five Gait isn't cooking."

Jeremiah glanced over the list his mother had sent.

The old man turned to Cody. "I am grateful for your family taking in this young warrior. I know he has a good heart, but also a very big appetite. There is no family in Halt that I would rather have him stay with."

"Townie, I mean, Jeremiah and I have lots of fun together," Cody offered.

The old man stared out the front door of the gym at a sight known only to his memory. "It is a strange time indeed. The cowboys and the Indians—they are the only ones left in this land who understand each other. Come on, Jeremiah."

Then he paused to look at his grandson. "This summer we will ask the elders to give you a new name."

Cody caught the spark in Jeremiah's brown eyes.

What's 100 . . . 150 years, Lord? The two of them could be wearing buckskin and walking through the woods. In fact, they'd probably both enjoy that. Thanks for giving me a good friend like Townie.

"I'll be home later," Jeremiah called.

"Don't forget to ask him about the rifle and the note if you get a chance." Cody shielded each word with the palms of his hands.

Cody watched them leave the gym. Then he heard a soft voice filter down from the balcony. The words were, "Nice game, cowboy." But the tone sounded sad and pensive.

Startled, he stood back. He squinted his eyes at someone wearing a tie-dyed T-shirt, crouched up on the top row with her long legs tucked under her.

"Feather? You were here all along? But why didn't you . . . What's going on?"

She looked down at her feet and didn't respond.

Cody took the narrow wooden stairs two at a time. It had been a year since he had been in the balcony of the Halt High School gym. He had forgotten how confined it was and how musty it smelled.

"Feather, what's wrong?" He bent low and tried to force her to look at him. She turned away and stared toward the basket next to the stage at the opposite end of the gym where the Porcupines and the Rams had already begun their contest.

"Is it your mom?" Cody asked. "Did she have another spell? Is that why you couldn't make it to the game on time?"

"I was here," she murmured.

"Here? Up here for the whole game? Why? We really missed you!"

"You won easily, it looked like."

"Oh, yeah, we won, but the point is, we missed you. Even Larry was worried about you. What's the matter? What happened? We didn't do something dumb again, did we?"

"No, it wasn't you guys. I just didn't feel like playing basketball." She still refused to look at him.

"Are you sick?" Suddenly Cody felt his face flush red. "Oh," he blurted out, "it's not that monthly girl thing, is it?"

I can't believe I said that. If I have to die, this would be a real good time! I don't even know what I'm talking about. Why did I say that?

"I wish it were that simple." Feather struggled to hold back the tears. "Mom says we're going to move, Cody!"

"Move? You mean, like leave the area? But you just moved here this spring. You can't move. We need you on our team and—"

"You can win without me."

"But you're . . . a friend. You're our friend, Feather. We don't want you to move. Where will you go?"

"Mother decided we should be up at Dixie with Dad to help protest the logging. Besides, if we go up there, we'll both be paid twenty-four dollars a day plus food."

"But I thought the plan was to have you two stay here."

"Well . . . plans change." Feather's voice sounded as flat as one of the computer voices that whines, "If you'd like to place an order, press 1 now."

"You'd be gone the whole summer?"

"Yeah. In fact, if Dad can find a cabin, we might stay there all winter, too."

"You mean move for good? This is horrible!" Cody moaned.

"Tell me about it."

"Can't you change your mother's mind?"

"I don't think so." Feather took a big, deep breath and wiped her eyes on her multicolored sleeve.

"Maybe you can spend the summer with someone here in Halt. You could live in town and play basketball and—"

"Who with? You guys have Jeremiah already."

Cody scratched the back of his head. "Well, there must be something we can do."

"I can't think of anything," Feather replied.

"We can pray." Cody dropped his chin to his chest. "Lord, this is my friend Feather, and her mom wants her to move away. Well, Lord, we sure like having her on our team and wondered if You had time, could You sort of think about it and maybe figure out a way Feather could stay in Halt at least through the summer? Thanks, Lord. In Jesus' name, amen."

He looked up. Feather's tear-streaked red eyes looked back at him. He felt himself blush again.

Lord, I think I meant that prayer to be just between You and me.

"That's how you pray?" she quizzed.

"D-did I do something wrong?" he stammered.

"Don't you use *thy* and *thou* and *howbeit* and all of that?"

Cody's eyes were fixed on hers. "What?"

"Nothing. It's just that I never thought prayer was like talking to someone."

"Am I doing it wrong?" Cody asked.

"No, no, that's not it. I just always thought that prayer was supposed to be a more, you know, formal thing."

"I guess you can do it any way you want, as long as you're talking to the right One. Does your mom want to move right away?"

"Saturday."

"This Saturday? That's only three days away!"

"She says there's no reason to wait. We'll just cram the VW bus with our belongings, tie down the flap on our tepee, and ride off."

"Well . . . three days. We'll just have to figure out the riddle of the rifle and how you can play in the basketball game on Friday and—"

"And your prayer will have to be answered." Feather scooted her legs out from under her.

They both sat in the bleachers and watched the two games going on in the gym. Cody thought of ten zillion things to say.

But none seemed to fit.

Cody was watching a television rerun of the Santa Maria, California, Elks' Rodeo when Jeremiah Yellowboy bounded through the door of the Clark home.

"Where is everyone?" Jeremiah quizzed.

"Dad's at a cattle breeder's meeting. Mom's downstairs doing the laundry, and Denver's at Becky's, of course."

"Did you find out what happened to Feather?"

"Yeah," Cody replied. "What about your grandpa? Did you learn anything about that gun?"

"I sure did. Is Feather's mother all right?"

"It wasn't her mother. Well, she isn't sick or anything. What did your grandad say the note meant?"

"He didn't even know it was in there. He never uses the wooden cleaning rods. He has a big, long metal one. If her mom wasn't sick, why'd Feather miss the game?"

"She didn't miss it. She was up in the bleachers all along. Could the note have been shoved in there by someone else in your family?"

"Hey, that's just it. I thought that the rifle had been in my family all along. But it hadn't. What do you mean, she was up in the bleachers? She purposely didn't play?"

"She said she didn't feel like it," Cody reported. "So who owned the rifle before your family?"

"I guess my great-grandfather pawned it right before World War II. Is Feather sick?"

"Not physically sick. She's just very, very depressed. You mean, your great-grandfather got a few bucks for the gun and left it at a pawn shop?"

"Yeah. According to Grandpa, they needed the money for groceries. But when Grandpa got out of the army after the war in 1945, he went down and got it out of hock. What's Feather depressed about?"

"Her mother said they're going to move up to Dixie to be with her father. You mean that gun sat in the pawn shop for six or seven years?"

"Actually, someone bought it, kept it a few years, and

then brought it back to the shop. When is she going to move?"

"This Saturday! Can you believe it? We've got to figure out something, Townie. She doesn't want to go up there. Hey, who was it that owned the rifle in the forties?"

"Grandpa doesn't know, but he said Chad Levine would remember. Eh . . . maybe Feather could stay here, too! You could give her Prescott's room."

"I couldn't ask my mom to do that. Haying season is coming up, and she'll have a crew to cook for, plus you and me and Denver at home, and work a couple days a week at the post office. Is it the old man Levine who has the sheep and goats down on the river breaks?"

"Yeah. He used to run a pawn shop right on Main Street—where the Groom & Loom is—in the late thirties and forties. Listen, I'm only going to be staying at your house until my mom comes home in two weeks. If Feather didn't move for a couple weeks, I'd be out of here."

"Yeah, maybe we could see if her mom will wait until the Fourth of July or something. I get the feeling that Feather doesn't have many friends." Cody flipped off the television. "Townie, did you ever ride your bike down to the river breaks?"

"One time me and Two Ponies rode down there to fish with my grandpa, but he brought us home in his truck. Coming home is the tough part. It's all uphill. You think we ought to ride down there? You know, I was thinking, Feather has it rough. It would be pretty lonely being an only child and then living out in the woods in a tepee. It's too isolated for even me," Jeremiah confessed.

"She's a bulldog though. If I had to choose sides in a scrape, I'd rather have Feather on my side than against me." Cody led the way to the kitchen. "Let's ride down to the breaks tomorrow and see if Old Man Levine can remember who bought that rifle. Whoever it was, I'll bet he was the one who put the note in the stock."

"Yeah, that's what Grandpa said. He didn't write it, and his father, who had the gun before him, always wrote in Nez Perce. Great-grandpa was real proud of being able to write. He refused to write anything in English. Shall we ask Larry and Feather to go with us?"

"I suppose they'd be pretty steamed if we went off without them. I think we ought to ask Mrs. Grossly to open the Halt Museum, too. They have a lot about the bombing of the bank in there. You want something to drink?"

"Sure. You have any more of those white-chocolate-covered Oreos?" Jeremiah pulled a carton of milk out of refrigerator and plopped it on the counter. "Larry's going to want us to practice tomorrow."

"We can practice in the afternoon. If we aren't too tired." Cody tossed a bag of cookies across the kitchen counter. "There aren't many left."

"I might as well finish them off," Jeremiah said. "Listen, with all that bike-riding tomorrow, maybe we should head to bed pretty soon."

"I'll need to go out and feed the horses early."

"Well, how about you doing it on your own? I don't think I was created to ride a bike all day long."

"Yellowboy, tell me the truth—what *were* you created to do all day long?"

"Besides eat?"

"Yeah."

"Dance. I was created to dance to the sound of the drums all night and all day. I never get tired of that. Grandpa says it's something in my bones. Once I get started, I can go on forever. How about you, Cody? What were you created to do all day long? Besides talking to the Lord."

"Ridin' and ropin', I guess. I've never had a day where I did it too much." Cody took a big gulp from a wide-mouth Mountain Dew. "I know how Larry would answer that question."

"Basketball!" Jeremiah howled. "That guy could shoot baskets day and night. I bet he dreams of basketball."

"Not just basketball, but winning basketball!" Cody laughed.

Jeremiah made his voice sound higher-pitched. "If you're going to be a winner, you've got to dream like a winner!"

Both boys roared. When they finally got control, Cody said, "But I really like Larry. Did you ever see anyone work so hard at winning?"

"Not since Geronimo," Jeremiah teased. "And what about Feather? What one thing was she created to do all day long?"

"I have a feeling," Cody sighed, "that not even Feather Trailer-Hobbs could answer that question."

Six

I don't want to talk about it!" Feather insisted.

"You're going to be moving away forever in three days, and you don't want to talk about it?" Cody coasted along beside her as the quartet bicycled down the gravel road toward the Salmon River breaks.

"Every minute I'm depressed over leaving is one less minute to enjoy being here. I want to treasure them all, so don't ask me about moving. Just pretend that I'm going to be around forever."

"What I can't figure out is how I ever let you talk me into this trip." Jeremiah put on his hand brakes so he wouldn't sail on past the others. "Look at how steep this is. There's no way to pedal out of here."

"You mean we might be trapped down at Mr. Levine's the rest of our lives?" Cody squeezed the rear brakes and slowed down just a tad.

"No, but I guarantee we'll be four tired puppies when we get back home! Too tired to practice basketball, that's for sure," Jeremiah predicted.

"No way!" Larry protested. "I only agreed to this because Cody said it was a good stamina and endurance exercise. And if our team drops to only three, then we'll have to push hard for the whole game instead of sitting out and getting our breath."

Cody looked over at Feather. She was biting down on her lower lip.

"We could talk over our game plan for tomorrow night's game as we ride," Larry suggested.

"Ahhhh!" Jeremiah moaned loud and long.

"Of course, if you'd rather I didn't explain it to you, just say so."

Feather, Cody, and Jeremiah echoed in unison a resounding, "So!"

"Hey, that was funny." Larry grinned. "But I'm serious. If you don't want to go over the game plan, we can wait until practice. But if we do it now, it will save time later, and we'll be able to do more drills. That sounds cool, doesn't it?"

"Nope," Cody shot back.

"You guys goof off so much I never know when you're serious. Listen, the Yellowjackets—we play them tomorrow night, remember?—well, they can't hit squat from the outside, so I developed—"

"Larry! We do not want to talk about basketball!" Cody hollered as they coasted down the grade.

"You mean it?"

"Yes!" Jeremiah screamed like someone who'd spent the day in the library whispering and finally stepped outside to clear the carbon buildup out of his lungs.

"Well, now, there's one vote." Larry nodded. The seat of his borrowed bicycle was a little too high and forced him almost to stand part of the time. "What about you, Feather? Do you want to talk about our game plan for tomorrow night?"

"Nope."

"Think about it for a minute. You know, it could be . . . your last game with the Squad, and I'm sure you want to make it a memorable win."

"She said no, Larry!" Cody insisted, swerving to the right to miss a football-sized rock that had tumbled into the roadway.

"Okay, that's two votes against discussing our game plan. And I vote in favor. Boy, have I got us a great play for scoring some quick points. Of course, it would help if one of us could slam dunk. Two to one. It looks like you have the decisive vote, Cody, my man. What do you say?" Larry pumped hard until he was out in front of the others.

"What do I say? I say Feather and Townie are right. I vote with them."

"What you're saying is that we shouldn't discuss our basketball game plan now?"

"You ever notice how quick a mind Larry has?" Jeremiah teased. "He catches on instantly."

"You know," Feather smiled wider than she had in several days, "my mother always warned me to watch out for boys with one-track minds. I wonder if this is what she was talking about?"

"Very funny." Larry quit his downhill pumping and came alongside the others. "I'm not a one-track person.

Let's talk about . . . about . . . Well, let's talk about what we're going to do when we get down to this guy Levine's place. What then?"

"We'll ask him to tell us everything he can remember about the man who purchased Mr. Yellowboy's rifle during the war. And then we'll cool our feet in the river, get a drink, and crank our way back up the mountain," Cody explained.

"Will we mention about the note?" Feather asked.

"Sure. Why not? Maybe he has some idea about it."

The pine, firs, spruce, and cedar of the mountains began to give way to granite boulders and sparse brown grass as they descended toward the river. It was a gradual rolling grade with only a couple of hairpin turns.

Cody felt the cool mountain breeze disappear as the stale heat of the canyon radiated off the gravel road. Cemetery Creek was almost dry, but thick green brush lined its banks. With clear blue sky and bright summer sun above, he wished he had worn a baseball cap like Jeremiah and Larry. His black sleeveless T-shirt was beginning to absorb an increasing amount of heat. Below them, deep in the canyon to the south, he spotted the blue and white sparkling reflection of the Salmon River.

"There it is!" Cody called out. "The River of No Return."

"This driveway might be the Road of No Return if it gets any steeper," Jeremiah griped.

"Where's Mr. Levine's place?" Larry asked.

"We'll turn left at the steamboat," Cody instructed.

"The steamboat?" Larry gasped. "How in the world did a steamboat get way up here?"

"Like Noah's Ark, it was washed up into the mountains during the Great Flood," Jeremiah announced with a grin.

"Really?" Larry slowed his bike almost to a stop.

"Not quite," Cody admitted. "One spring about 100 years ago, during really high water, they brought a steamboat up the Snake River to the Salmon and then past here to Six Mile Rapids, where they unloaded supplies and loaded up on gold. But on the return trip, the water was going down fast, and they only got here to Cemetery Creek when they started to break up on the rocks."

Cody pulled over and stopped his bike next to the hull of the *Pride of Astoria*. The others followed his lead. "I guess they got it to shore but lost a lot of the cargo. Then a few years later, during a flood year, the river changed course and left the boat over here."

"Lost gold! All right! Why don't we rent some scuba gear and come down here and—," Larry began. "See! See, I'm talking about something besides basketball! I told you I could do it."

"You're terrific," Cody jibed. "Come on, Squad, time for a little pedaling." He turned east and began to pedal up the narrow, rutted dirt road. He kept changing gears on Denver's bike, trying to find one he could manage.

"Someone actually lives up this road?" Feather gasped between breaths.

"I came down here one time with my mom when I was about five. She had a bunch of mail for Mr. Levine at Christmas. He hadn't been to town for a couple months, so she came to check on him."

"Was he all right?" she asked.

"Yeah. He said the Christmas crowds were just too much for him."

"Christmas crowds in Halt?"

"That's what I said."

The road became so steep that Cody jumped off his bike and began to push it up the hill. The others did the same.

"How come a man who ran a business downtown suddenly decided to move out here and be a hermit?" Larry asked as he pushed and puffed his way up the hill.

"Mother said it had something to do with the death of his wife. I don't know if she was sick or what. Anyway, he took it hard and moved out here on the breaks in the early 1950s."

"That sounds weird," Larry remarked.

"It sounds perfectly logical to me," Feather shot back. "If a person wants to move out into some remote area, they certainly have the right to do so without everyone calling them weird!"

"Eh . . . yeah, whatever," Larry stammered.

"There's his place." Cody pointed off to the south.

"That log cabin?" Jeremiah exclaimed.

Cody gazed on up the sloping Salmon River Canyon. "Yep, and he's got a great view. Sure makes us seem small way down here, doesn't it?"

"What if he isn't home?" Larry asked.

"We'll wait," Cody replied.

"What if he doesn't come back until September?" Jeremiah pressed.

"Then we'll have time to go over Larry's game plans."

Larry looked Cody right in the eyes. "Really?"

"Hey, there he is! Over by that mule in the corral. Hello, Mr. Levine," he called.

The stoop-shouldered, white-haired man with grizzled beard and cane turned around. His bushy gray eyebrows raised in surprise.

"Oh . . . my . . . I wasn't expecting company."

They left their bikes in front of the cabin, and Cody led the group out to the old man.

"Mr. Levine, I'm Cody Clark—Margaret and Hank Clark's youngest."

"Well, so you are. And I'm Chadnezzar Sylmann Levine, Abraham and Deborah's eldest. It's good to see you again, young Mr. Clark. It's been about eight years, hasn't it?"

"Yes, sir."

"Well, you should stop by more often. I trust you didn't bring my mail down. I was planning on going to town in a week or so. There was no need for you to come out."

"No, sir, we didn't bring any mail. We, eh, wanted to talk about the old days of Halt," Cody explained, "when you ran the pawn shop. I never knew before that you ran a pawn shop."

"The old days? Hah! Those weren't the old days. The 1890s and 1900—*those* were the old days. By the time I got to Halt, the place had calmed down considerably. Of course, by then the mines had played out, and lumber mills just about all went broke during the Depression. But there were some good times."

The old man stared out over the river to the distant rise

of the uninhabited Joseph Plains. "And there were some tragic times . . . terrible tragic times," he mumbled. Then he looked back at the kids. "My-oh-my, where is my hospitality? I have not even offered you some shade. May God forgive me. Come, come, let's go into the house. I have some spring water that is the coldest, purest water in the entire state of Idaho. If I bottled it, I could put Perrier out of business in a month."

They trailed along behind the old man, who wore a long-sleeved white shirt with dirty collar buttoned tight and black wool trousers worn slick in the seat and the knees. "Strawberries. I'll fix us all some very fine Salmon River strawberries and fresh cream. Why, of course." Then he looked up at the sky. "Mama, I am getting old. Children coming to visit, and I didn't think of feeding them. I'm ashamed."

Feather rolled her eyes at Cody.

Chad Levine's house was just one room. But it was a very large room—almost like a barn. The windows ran from floor to ceiling all along the south side, offering a spectacular view of the river and canyon. Newspapers from around the world were neatly stacked in old wooden apple crates that lined the north wall. Cody was surprised at how clean and orderly everything looked.

Jeremiah caught Cody's attention and pointed frantically at a worn cardboard shoe box on the arm of a homemade leather-cushioned oak sofa.

Cody felt his heart skip a beat.

Hundred dollar bills? A whole shoe box with neatly filed hundred dollar bills!

He and Jeremiah joined Larry and Feather at the wall of windows. All four kids stared at the view while Mr. Levine busied himself at the kitchen counter, which seemed to take up the entire west wall of the room.

"Did you ever see anything like this?" Larry sounded sincerely impressed.

"I call it the Almighty's backyard," Mr. Levine called.

"Why?" Feather asked.

"Well, I can look for 100 to 200 miles in three directions and not see a single object made by man. Not a power pole, not a road, not a building—nothing! Don't you think the Almighty's backyard must look like that?"

"Yes, sir." Cody nodded. "I reckon you're right."

"Come on, we will sit out on the porch and eat strawberries. Young Mr. Yellowboy—you are a Yellowboy, aren't you?"

"Yes, sir," Jeremiah gulped. "How did you know?"

"Because you look just like your father and your grandfather."

"I do?"

"Most certainly. Would you scoot out some chairs? Now, young lady, these boys are too bashful to act civil. I don't believe we've been introduced."

"I'm Feather . . . Feather Trailer-Hobbs." She reached out and shook the old man's gnarly yet strong hand.

"Are you new around here?"

"Yes, sir. I live—well, we might be moving, but I live out on the old stage road southwest of Halt."

"Do you live in the tepee?"

"Yes, sir. How did you know about it?"

"Your father came to see me last spring before you and your mother moved out. Asked my advice about living in the tepee."

"What did you tell him?" Larry asked.

"He stood right here in this cabin when I told him to set it up next to the breaks, and he could last most every winter. I warned him that on the old stage road you could not possibly stay through October. But I knew he wouldn't listen to me. Which is all right. I am used to people not listening to me."

"My name's Larry Lewis. My dad's the new high school basketball coach," Larry blurted out.

Mr. Levine brought out a huge wooden bowl full of freshly washed whole strawberries. Then he handed them each a small china saucer. Circling the group, he poured cream from a bright stainless steel one-gallon container into each saucer.

"Let me show you how to eat strawberries." The old man dipped the strawberry halfway into the cream. Then he ate that half and proceeded to dunk the second half and eat it.

Soon all four were diving into the bowl of strawberries and dipping the thick cream from their saucers.

"Now what was so important that four very brave young people bicycled all the way to the breaks to see me?"

Cody cleared his throat. "Oh, we just got curious about the old days of Halt. . . . Well, I mean the thirties and forties mainly. Townie, eh, Jeremiah's grandad said you knew all about those days. He said you had a pawn shop right downtown. I always thought you were born and raised out here."

"On the breaks? God should so bless. No, I was born and raised in Chicago. I inherited the house of my grand-parents but couldn't keep a job during the Depression. So I sold the house. We brought the money with us on a train, stuffed in a shoe box—can you imagine that? We arrived in Halt, and I bought the old dry goods store and started a pawn shop. I had thought about starting a bank, but the regulations were too strict by then. The pawn shop was a good business. People were hurting for grocery money. I could help them and make a little profit for myself. It's not like that today. In the big cities, the pawn shops are just places for drug addicts to sell stolen mer-chandise."

"What was it like in Halt when all those businesses were open on Main Street?" Feather asked. "I saw the pic-tures down at the post office."

"We stayed open until after the 11:00 P.M. shift at the mill. All the businesses stayed open. People in the street all hours of the day and night. It was very busy—perhaps too busy."

Cody noticed that Mr. Levine stared out at the canyon a lot as he talked.

"Why did you give up that business and come out here?" Feather asked.

"When I lost Mama, it just took the heart out of me. I needed to be alone. I needed time to think. I needed time to read . . . so I came out here with a hundred ewes, three rams, and two dogs. I came just for a season of reflection. But I never left. That was forty-four years ago . . ." His voice trailed off. Then he turned to Larry. "Say, did you ever hear how Halt got its name?"

"Eh, Jeremiah and Cody told me one time about all the stage robberies and stuff."

"The what?"

"The old grade up the mountains and—"

"Well, certainly there was a winding road, but there were no stage holdups."

Larry frowned at Cody.

"We just sort of made that part up!" Cody grinned back.

"You see," the old man explained, "the grade was so steep and curving that the stagecoach passengers would get sick and yell 'Halt' when they finally reached a wide enough place to pull over at the top of mountains. Pretty soon the drivers just began to call the site Halt—because someone was sure to holler it on every trip. They say more than one Lewiston breakfast was lost at Halt. So when the first stage stop was built, they just called it Halt."

Larry listened intently. Mr. Levine winked at Cody. Then he looked at Jeremiah. "Young Mr. Yellowboy, how is your grandfather? He didn't come fishing with me this spring."

"He was sick for quite a while," Jeremiah reported. "But he is fine now."

"Did he ever tell you about the time we were in my little boat on the river and he gaffed a sturgeon? It was so big we thought it would capsize the boat. We finally pulled it ashore down at New Philadelphia beach. It was eleven feet long and weighed almost 300 pounds. I don't suppose there are many of those big boys out in the river anymore."

Cody finished the last of his strawberries. "Mr. Levine, I have a question for you."

"Oh, here it comes. Now I find out why you came to visit an old shepherd."

"Well, sir, we were looking at Jeremiah's grandad's '73 Winchester rifle the other day and—"

"Round barrel, first model, serial number around 21,000, with all the brass tacks in the stock—yes, I remember it. Your great-grandfather hated to part with it. But those were lean days. I gave him ten dollars. I think he used it all for flour, beans, coffee, and sugar. I was delighted to sell it back to your grandfather after the war."

A black-and-white dog trotted up to the porch, sniffed everyone, and then settled in next to Feather as she stroked its head.

"Mr. Levine, did you sell the gun to someone else during the war?" Cody asked.

"Yes, right before the war actually. Mr. Yellowboy told me to sell it because he didn't think he could ever buy it back. I sold it to the Italians for eighteen dollars. . . . Then the night they all moved, I bought it back for five dollars."

"The Italians?" Cody asked.

"Out east of town, two Italian families moved in to homestead down in Stinking Water Canyon."

"Stinking Water Canyon?" Cody echoed.

"Cougar Canyon. . . . They call it Cougar Canyon now. Well, the Italians lived there several years, and then one night they packed up all their supplies, came to town and sold off what they could, and took the train to San Francisco. I bought several nice items from them. The Yellowboy rifle I just stuck in my safe and waited for one of the family to come in looking for it."

"Do you remember when the Italians left?"

"I don't remember the exact day. It was not long after the jail got bombed."

"Whoa! They left soon after the jail was bombed?" Larry exclaimed.

"Yes. I don't forget. I don't forget anything. You know, so many old people lament their loss of memory. But a slight memory loss is a blessing. There are too many things in my life that I wish I could forget—but can't."

"What was the Italian family's name?" Larry asked.

"One was DeLira and the other Miritzi. They were related, but I never knew exactly how. It was Mr. DeLira who bought the gun, but I assumed both families used it. Why do you ask?"

"Well," Jeremiah confided, "inside the cleaning rod hole in the stock of Grandpa's rifle, we found a very old note that we think one of the Italians might have written."

"A note? What did it say?"

"'A + B + C + D = God is just,'" Feather reported.

The old man stared out across the canyon. "Indeed He is . . . indeed He is," he mumbled. "That's strange. Did you know that after the bombing, someone wrote those same words on the old jail? Look for yourself. There is a picture of it at the post office."

"We saw that yesterday," Feather told him.

They finished their strawberries and said good-bye to

Mr. Levine. It was almost noon when they started their trek out of his drive to Cemetery Creek Road.

It was 3:30 P.M. when they made it back to Cody's house and collapsed on the front steps. By then not even Larry Bird Lewis wanted to practice basketball.

Seven

Socks Bar is a golden chestnut standing at 15.5 hands.

Nickels is a blue roan, 14.5 at best.

Rolly is a buckskin dun over 16.5.

And Lawyer is a piebald standing at 15 even.

All four have mostly quarter horse bloodlines.

All four belong to the Clark family.

And by 10:00 A.M. Friday, Cody had all four saddled and waiting by the barn when his seventeen-year-old brother Denver drove up in his pickup truck with the rest of the Lewis and Clark Squad in the back.

"So you're riding horses today," Denver yelled.

"Yep. I'm usin' your old saddle. Is that okay?" Cody hollered.

"Just put it up when you're done."

"Thanks for the ride, Denver," Feather drawled, hanging around the open pickup window.

"Anytime, Feather girl. Just don't ride Lawyer."

"Which one is he?"

"The black-and-white one."

"He's pretty."

"Ask Cody why we call him Lawyer." Denver waved to the others and then raised a cloud of dust on his way out of the yard.

"We really are going to ride horses?" Larry gasped.

"It's cool. Even *you* will like it," Jeremiah encouraged him. "I get Socks!"

"Which one is that?" Larry asked.

"The one with the two white ankles," Cody reported. "Feather, would you like to ride Nickels?"

"Oh, sure, give the tallest person the shortest horse." She folded her arms and scowled.

"He's the smartest horse we own. I thought you might enjoy him."

"Oh, well, if he's the smartest, that fits." She smiled.

"What do you mean, that fits?" Larry pressed. "Do you mean to say that you're the smartest of the four of us? Listen, I've gotten nothing but A's for years! How can you beat straight A's?"

"Grades? You think intelligence is measured by a letter on a slip of paper assigned by a government employee whose main concern is looking after their retirement income? Grades are meaningless." Feather shuffled her left foot into the stirrup and swung into the saddle of the blue roan.

"Old Rolly's my horse." Cody patted the dun horse on the neck. "So that leaves you with Lawyer." He nodded to Larry. "You guys mount up, and I'll check the cinches."

"All right! I get the fancy one," Larry shouted. "Let's see now . . . how did you do that?"

"Stick your left foot in the stirrup, grab the saddle horn with your left hand, and then pull yourself up," Jeremiah instructed.

Soon all four were mounted. It felt strange to Cody to be wearing his basketball shoes instead of boots. *At least I did remember my cowboy hat!*

"Now, look, we aren't going to try anything fancy. Just a simple little trail ride because—" He glanced over at Feather. "—one of us is moving tomorrow, and a couple weeks ago I promised we would take a trail ride this summer. So I like to keep every promise."

"Where are we going?" Jeremiah asked.

"Cougar Canyon," Cody told them.

"Where those Italians used to live?" Feather asked.

"Yep. Thought we might as well take a look down there. It's been pretty much abandoned for years."

"We need to practice basketball today," Larry reminded him. "We missed yesterday, and we have a big game tonight."

"As soon as we return. You ready to ride, partners?" Cody called.

"Head 'em out!" Jeremiah hollered and kicked Socks Bar in the side.

"Just walk him to start with," Cody yelled. "And no galloping, Yellowboy!"

Jeremiah rode the horse out toward the gravel road. Feather punched her basketball shoes into the blue roan. "Come on, boy, giddyup!"

Cody waited for Larry to follow, but he just sat there.

"Go ahead, Larry. I'll follow."

"Eh . . . how do you, you know, get him going?"

"I thought you said you'd ridden before."

"That was in preschool. The guy led the horse around the play yard."

"Just kick him a little with your heels and say, 'Giddyup.' He'll go. If you want to go to the right, pull the reins gently to the right. Left, pull to the left. And if you want him to stop, holler, 'Whoa,' and pull straight back."

Larry began to relax. "This is really cool. You think my basketball will be all right next to the corrals?"

"I'm sure it will miss you, but it will be just fine!" Cody teased.

"Okay, well . . . here goes."

Larry pulled his heels a good two feet away from the horse and slammed them into his side.

"No!" Cody yelled.

"Giddyup!" Larry hollered.

Lawyer bucked straight forward and then immediately stopped.

But Larry didn't.

He tumbled over the horse's head and landed with a crash on the dirt.

Cody jumped off his horse. He reached down to help Larry to his feet.

"What happened?" Larry shook his head back and forth and then brushed the red soil out of his blond hair.

"You hit him too hard. You've got to be gentle with Lawyer. Now hop back on there and try it again."

"Get back on there? You've got to be kidding."

"Hey, when you have a bike wreck, you go on riding a bike, don't you?"

"Eh, yeah, but—"

"Go on. Once Lawyer takes a liking to you, he's a very steady horse."

"I really have to climb back up there?"

"It builds character."

"You sound like my dad," Larry grumbled. He cautiously remounted the black-and-white horse.

"You promise he won't buck this time?"

"Just barely touch him with your heels."

Larry did so, and the piebald began a steady walk past the corrals toward the road. "All right, now I've got it!" Larry shouted in triumph.

"Well, there's a few more things to learn."

They caught up with Feather and Jeremiah in front of Eureka Blaine's driveway.

"Are you all right?" Feather called out.

"Oh, yeah." Larry was still brushing the dust off his shirt.

"Larry and Lawyer just needed to come to a little understanding, that's all," Cody informed them.

"Hey, Denver said I should ask you to tell me why that horse is called Lawyer," Feather remembered.

"Oh, it's because no matter who you are or what you've done, he'll figure a way to get you off."

"Funny! Oh, very funny! You cripple me, Clark, and you and Townie will have the only two-man team in the three-on-three league!" Larry clutched the saddle horn with his right hand and the reins in his left.

By the time they reached Cougar Canyon, Larry was gripping the saddle horn with both hands, and Feather was standing in the stirrups.

"Now as far as I can remember what Grandpa told me . . . the Italians homesteaded from the road clear down to the mouth of the canyon. There were two families, and they had identical houses facing each other. Between the houses was a big outdoor kitchen that they used all year round. Both families used the same kitchen."

"Where is it?" Feather asked.

"It's all gone—houses, barns, arbors, vineyards."

"Vineyards? They tried growing grapes up here in the mountains?" Jeremiah marveled.

"That's what I hear."

"Wait a minute," Larry interjected. "If everything's gone and burned down, why did we come here?"

"Just for a ride and to look inside that circle of trees," Cody replied.

"What's in there?" Feather urged her horse toward the trees.

"That's what I've been wondering. Those tall ones are Italian Cypress. They were planted on purpose. But now they're so wild and overgrown you can't even see in, but there must be something in the midst of them. Townie, hold Rolly Boy for me."

Cody dismounted and pushed his way through the bramble. Bending low, he shoved each limb back gingerly, trying not to get his arms or legs scratched.

"What do you see?" Feather called out, still mounted.

Cody saw nothing but brush, so he didn't respond but

shoved his way out into the middle of the circle of extremely tall, skinny cypress trees.

These are so thick the cows can't even get in here to graze. 'Course, maybe that's why they planted them. There's nothing in here. Boy, this was a waste of time.

"Cody!" Feather called again. "Are you all right?"

"I'm fine! I can't find anything in here. Maybe they just—hey!"

Cody had stumbled over what he thought was a huge rock. Pulling back the weeds and dead brush, he discovered that someone had crudely chiseled words into the rock.

"What is it?" Feather called again.

"Hey, I found it. . . . It's like a homemade grave marker," he hollered.

"Does it say, 'God is just'?" she quizzed.

"Nope."

"I'll come help you look," Feather yelled.

She fought her way through the brush to Cody's side.

"How many have you found?" she asked.

"Just this one in the center of the trees."

"Wow, look at that. 'Dola Maria DeLira, 1930-1939.' She was only nine years old, Cody."

The sound of a person crashing through the bushes caused Cody and Feather to spin around.

"Hey, what's happening in here?" Jeremiah sputtered. "This is weird. A private cemetery?"

"It's kind of sad-looking, all overgrown," Feather observed. "Maybe we should clean the brush back."

"Yeah," Cody agreed. "I'll break off these limbs. Townie,

you pull the weeds." He glanced up to see Feather scooting out of the ring of trees. "Where are you going?"

"To pick some wildflowers."

Ten minutes later the grave was a tiny wildflower-strewn patch in the midst of thirty-foot Italian Cypress trees.

"I'm glad we did that." Feather grinned. Her normally pale complexion had taken on a red tint from the bright summer sun. "It always feels good when you know you did the right thing."

"Whoa!" Larry's shrill scream was followed by a loud thud and a long groan. The sound of hooves hitting hard dirt sickened Cody.

"Hey, what did you do with the horses?"

"I let Larry hold them," Jeremiah explained.

Oh, no, not the horses . . . Oh, man, not today. I don't need this, Lord—not the horses!

When they broke into the clearing, Larry was lying in the weeds, his foot tangled in the reins. Lawyer grazed next to him. The other three horses were just a cloud of dust across the prairie.

"Look after Larry. I'll go get the horses," Cody yelled as he jerked the reins from Larry's foot and mounted the piebald gelding. He slammed his heels into Lawyer, and the horse bucked twice before tearing off after the other horses.

Rolly waited for him at the top of the first prairie roll. Nickels was drinking water from Carpenters' stock tank, and Socks Bar was nowhere in sight.

Socksy went home. He gets scared, he goes home. One of us will have to double up. Lord, I sure hope Larry didn't get hurt. It's all my fault. I got too busy with that old ceme-

tery. *That's enough mystery for now. We'll go practice and then rest up for the game. This is crazy.*

Cody found all three waiting for him near the driveway that led to the old Italian homestead. Jeremiah wore his Bulls cap backwards. Feather had stuck some wildflowers in her long brown ponytail, and Larry had dirt smeared across his arms, face, and knees.

"Larry, are you all right?"

"The NBA has been spared the tragic grief of losing one of their future superstars at an early age."

"Where's Socks?" Jeremiah asked.

"He got disgusted with the whole deal and went home."

"By himself?" Larry asked.

"He's a big boy—he won't get lost," Cody assured him. "Townie, you ride Rolly for me. I've got Lawyer calmed down, so I'll stay up here. But I don't think he'll ride double. Larry, hop up there with Townie. Rolly's plenty big for both of you."

"Oh, no, you slammed me into the ground twice in the same morning, Clark. I'm not going to let you do it again."

"You going to walk all the way back?"

"Maybe I'll jog part of the way—provided all my body parts are still working."

By the time they reached the Clark barn, groomed the horses, including Socks Bar, and turned them out to pasture, Larry Lewis was zonked out in the hay near the open loft.

"Let him sleep," Cody told the other two.

"But how can we practice without the coach?" Jeremiah asked.

"Why don't we just shoot around and then try a couple two-on-one drills?" Feather suggested.

"Sounds good to me." Cody began to rebound and pass the ball back out to Feather and Jeremiah, who kept shooting three-pointers.

"Thanks for the trail ride, Cody," Feather called between shots.

"Sorry we had trouble with the horses," he responded, passing the ball out to her.

She fired up a set shot that bounced high on the iron rim. "It was fun, but I don't think we are any closer to solving the riddle of the rifle."

"Yeah. I figure it's probably easy to explain . . . if a person knew all the facts." Cody took the rebound and bounce-passed it to Jeremiah.

"But sometimes the facts are pretty boring, you know what I mean?" Feather added. "At least we did clean up that grave site. It wasn't a total waste of time."

Jeremiah's shot hit nothing but net.

"Yeah, when we don't know why something happened, we can imagine all sorts of things." Cody took the ball and tried a right hand hook shot from five feet.

Nothing but air.

"Remind me not to try that in the game," he laughed. "Listen, Feather, Townie and I were talking, and we thought it would be fun after the game to have a little party at my house. You know, a going-away party for you. Is that—"

"No!" she cried.

"Come on, Feather, we don't want to . . . just say, 'Nice game, kid. See you around some year,' and leave it at that."

"I said, no party!" she repeated. "You know I don't want to go, so I'm really trying to work something out with my mom."

"You mean, you might be able to stay?" Cody spun around, but she turned her head to the side. He couldn't see her face.

"I just said I was working on something, that's all."

"That would be great. . . . Wouldn't it, Townie?"

"It sure would!" Jeremiah took the ball and flipped a right-handed hook shot from the three-point line. The ball flew fifteen feet right off the basket and into the open barn loft. "Whoa! Remind me not to try that shot during a game," he laughed.

"What's going on? . . . Are you guys starting practice without me? . . . Where in the practice are you?" Larry stood above them in the loft, clutching the basketball.

"We've gotten to the three-point shot shoot-around."

"Wow, you're almost through. I'll be right down." He tossed the ball down to Feather.

When he finally reached them, Larry staggered a little. "Boy, am I stiff. . . . Are you guys stiff? My legs can hardly move."

"We're doing okay, but you were the one who ran home from Cougar Canyon," Jeremiah reminded him.

"You know . . . I think—if you guys say it's all right— I think I'll sit out this practice. I'm glad we don't have to ride our bikes back to town. Denver is going to give us a lift, isn't he?"

The good news was that it was a Friday night basketball game, and they had the last of the three scheduled contests. That meant the biggest crowd of the week would be in the gym. Cody figured over 200 family members, friends, and neighbors had stopped by to watch the summer league contest.

That was also the bad news.

Lord, I don't know why I always blow it when other people are watching. Mom, Dad, Denver—everyone's here. If I could just do as well as I do in practice.

Feather hardly spoke to him when she arrived at the gym. She, Cody, and Jeremiah sat at the end of the bleachers and waited for the middle game to end. Larry Lewis hobbled in, dribbling his ball along the sidelines.

"Larry, you look horrible," Jeremiah commented.

"Yeah, and I feel worse. My legs keep cramping up every direction I turn. Dad said I should use the Jacuzzi in the high school weight room after the game."

"You can't play like that!" Cody told him.

"No . . . I'll be all right, once the adrenaline kicks in. I've got to play. I start every game. It's my signature. I can't break the string. All my life, on every team I've been on—from Little Dribblers to the junior high team—I've always started."

Cody glanced over at Jeremiah and Feather, then back at Larry. "Okay, but I'm running the team tonight," he declared. "Is that all right with you, Larry?"

"Yeah, yeah, you're going to get more minutes than me. That makes sense."

"Then here's the way it goes," Cody instructed. "Larry,

you, Feather, and Townie are starting. Feather will play post until I come in. Feather, if we bring it in, try that play where you drive right next to Townie, then slash to the basket, and dump the ball back to him. Townie, fire it over to Larry at the line, and he'll take a jumper. Right after that shot is made, call a time out."

"Wait a minute; I don't think—," Larry began.

"I'm the captain tonight, Lewis," Cody reminded him.

"Yes, sir," Larry replied.

When the game started, they ran the play exactly as planned, but Larry wasn't able to hobble up to the free-throw line. Instead, he stopped at the top of the key.

His shot circled the rim once, then fell in for a three-pointer. Feather immediately called time out.

"Larry, I'm coming in for you," Cody hollered. "Your minutes are over for tonight."

Larry just limped off. "Yeah. Thanks, Cody," he mumbled. "Now don't you guys lose my lead."

They didn't.

The game belonged to Feather.

She outjumped, outhustled, outstole, and outshot everyone on the court. Several times Cody and Jeremiah just stood and watched her with their hands on their hips.

A turn-around jumper of Feather's from the base line ended the game twenty to fourteen. Cody and Jeremiah raced off the court toward Larry, who sat on the bottom row of the bleachers dribbling his ball.

"Great game, you guys," he shouted. "Five and one—the Squad has the second-best record in the league."

"It was all Feather. You really—" Cody spun around to stare at the thinning crowd. "Where did she go?"

Jeremiah's eyes searched the gym. "Maybe she went out to get a drink."

"Anyway," Larry broke back in, "it shows that we have what it takes to win even when one of us is injured."

"Yeah, but one of us is moving tomorrow!" Cody reminded them, again looking around the gym. "Maybe she went to the girls' room. You didn't see her mom in the crowd, did you? I thought for sure her mom would come to *this* game, being the last and all."

Cody glanced up to see his mom, dad, and brother approaching.

"Nice game, little bro." Denver gave him a high five.

"Cody Wayne, did you say something inappropriate to Feather?" his mother grilled.

"Feather? No, ma'am. Didn't she play a great game?"

"Yes, she did," his mother replied. "That's why I was surprised that she ran out of the gym in tears."

Eight

Sometime during the night a summer storm swept through the Bitterroot Mountains and across the Camas Prairie. Cody faintly remembered the clap of thunder and the crack of lightning. It was, to his way of thinking, a perfect storm. There had been just enough rain to settle the dust, but not enough to make any mud. By morning it was sunny and beginning to warm up.

He slept late. He was sitting on the front step eating a bowl of Cheerios when he heard the phone ring.

Mom can get it.

On the fourth ring he leaped up and dashed inside.

This is Saturday. Mom's at the post office.

"Clark residence. Cody speaking."

"Cody Wayne, are you just getting up?"

"Mom! Eh, no, I was outside eating my cereal."

"What time were Feather and her mother going to leave today?"

"I don't know. I sort of figured early. But come to think about it, they don't seem like early people. Why?"

"Well, Feather got a letter from the production company that filmed the television commercial last week. It's probably the money they promised her. I was hoping to get it to her before she left."

"Can you forward it to Dixie?"

"No, because I don't have any mail forwarding card on file."

"What are we going to do?"

"I'm tied up here until noon, and your father and Denver are at cattle auction, so . . ."

"I could ride out there on my bike and take it to her," Cody offered.

"That's precisely what I was thinking. Finish your breakfast. Did you take a vitamin?"

"Eh, no, ma'am."

"Then do it. See you after a while, punkin'."

I am thirteen years old. I am not a punkin'—or a pumpkin.

The partially gravel, mostly dirt winding road to Feather's was completely empty of traffic. Cody breezed along with her letter folded and jammed in the back pocket of his Wranglers. Even though it was now a clear morning, the storm had brought cooler air to the mountains, and he wore his black National Finals Rodeo sweatshirt. His shaggy, dark brown hair blew in the wind, and he couldn't remember whether he had taken time to comb it.

I should have looked in the mirror. 'Course, it's not like Feather's my girlfriend or anything. I don't have a girlfriend.

*If I did have one, I'd want her to be . . . sort of like Feather
. . . only different.*

*She needs to be kind of halfway between Honey Del
Mateo and Feather. Of course, she's got to be a Christian.
And she needs to like horses and rodeos and not be afraid
to doctor a sick cow or too prissy to let a calf warm up in
the bathtub, and she should like basketball and cowboy
music and Dodge pickups and steaks medium rare, and like
to go deer-hunting, and she would not decorate the house
with pink wallpaper.*

And cute. Lord, she has to have an awesome smile.

Like Honey . . . and Feather.

The rope was stretched across the cattle guard
entrance to Feather's place. He unfastened it, pushed his
bike across, and refastened the rope. Then he pedaled up
the dirt drive. His heart sank when he saw the fresh car
tracks in the road. By the time he reached the tepee, it was
no surprise that the VW bus was gone, and the lodge door
was tied down tight.

He called out anyway but didn't bother getting off his
bike. "Feather! Feather, it's me—Cody. Are you home?"

*Do they just go off and leave this? Don't they come back
and pack up their tepee? Do they haul off this junk? Do they
keep the property or sell it?*

"Feather?"

*They can't use a tepee in Dixie. It goes down to forty
below with fifteen feet of snow there. I've only known her
a couple weeks, but we've been playing basketball about
every day. I think I'm going to miss her.*

I know I'm going to miss her.

The ride back to Halt seemed even longer. It was a relief when he rounded the bend and saw Expedition Lake. After struggling to climb the steep hill on the north side of the lake, Cody flew across town to report to his mother at the post office.

She told him to take the letter home and keep it a few days, in case they heard something from Feather. But before he went home, he decided to ride out to Eureka Blaine's and feed the horses.

Lord, feeding the neighbor's horses every day when he's gone is a good job, but sometimes it's kind of boring. Do You ever get bored of feeding us every day? I mean, every day—three times a day—gimme, gimme, gimme. I guess that's why we're supposed to say thanks before we eat, isn't it?

Other people would have called the ride scenic. But for Cody, it was just the same old thing. The light green of rolling hay fields, the red dirt roadways, the dark green forests, the deep blue unpolluted 4,000-foot elevation sky, the soaring white clouds, and the glare of a bright yellow sun.

It's summer on the high mountain prairie.

The cows moo, the birds chirp, the deer and elk crash through the forest, and the horses gallop across the pasture in flight from imaginary assailants.

Riding up Blaine's driveway, Cody gazed off to the east.

Lord, in the winter, it's like the weather is your enemy. It's something you fight every day just to break even. But in the summer, it's like we're both on the same side. People shouldn't move in the summer. It doesn't feel right.

Cody fed Eureka's string of horses, checked the hooves on the geldings, and climbed up on the corral fence to stare at the empty pasture.

Last week they were filming a Pizza Palace commercial right there—Bruce Baxter himself. Now it's just mashed timothy grass. Feather did really good, too. Lord, if You wanted her to, I bet she could be an actress someday. Or is it an actor?

Whatever. I can just hear her: "Thank you . . . thank you so much. . . . I'd like to thank all the members of the Academy for giving me this award. And I'd like to thank all you little people who made my fabulously lucrative career possible. And especially I'd like to thank Cody Wayne Clark who gave me my first break years ago when he declined a starring role in a Pizza Palace commercial and recognized my superior talents by allowing me to fill in. He was such a dear lad."

Cody jumped off the fence and sauntered over to the stock tank. He was just about ready to head to his bicycle. He leaned against a cottonwood tree in Eureka's yard, and then he noticed them.

Something inside him leaped. He couldn't help hollering, "Whoa! Look at those prints!"

The rain during the night had not only settled the dust in Eureka's backyard, but it had erased all previous tracks. The now-dry dirt fluffed up in such a way that every new impression was crisp and unsmeared. There in the dirt by the water faucet next to the stock tank—fresh prints.

Stocking feet?

About size seven or eight.

But nobody would kick off their shoes and just wear socks way out here. Unless someone's staying at Eureka's.

Which they aren't.

Mounting his bicycle, Cody rode back out Blaine's driveway to follow the tracks as they led across the gravel road, past the corrals, and into the dirt yard next to the Clark ranch barn.

They checked out our barn, too? Either they left the stock tank to come look in our barn, or they left the barn to go to the stock tank. But we have stock tanks over here, so why go to Eureka's? 'Course, he does have the best water, but nobody knows that unless . . .

Cody leaned his bike against the side of the barn and slowly pulled open the door. Peeking inside, he waited for his eyes to adjust to the semidarkness of the huge building. He could smell hay, leather, and manure.

He thought about shouting but felt a caution. He opted for slipping in unannounced instead. The dirt barn floor was too hard-packed and too dark to see any tracks at all.

Did someone sleep in the barn overnight? Back during the '70s Dad says he used to find people sleeping in the barn almost every week in the summer. But this isn't just anybody.

He approached the ladder to the massive loft and then thought of the tack room.

If they busted in and stole a saddle or something . . . not my roping saddle!

Pushing softly on the door, he could tell it was locked.

That's good. I'll just . . . but what if someone broke in, stole my saddle, and then locked it up so we wouldn't know for a few days. They could be clear out of the country before we even knew we lost anything.

Cody reached up behind a broken board in the barn wall and retrieved a worn brass key. Unlocking the tack room door, he shoved it with a hard push. The door banged open.

On an old army cot, near the unused woodstove, someone sat straight up in a green sleeping bag and shouted, "What are you doing in my room? Get out of here!"

Cody jumped back into the main part of the barn, slamming the door behind him.

"Feather?" he hollered.

"Cody?"

"What are you doing here?"

"I was trying to sleep. Before you woke me up."

"It's after nine in the morning."

"Well, I didn't sleep much last night, and I'm tired."

"But—but what are you doing here in our barn?"

"I told you I was trying to sleep. Is that all right with you?"

"Yeah, but you're moving today. . . . I mean, you moved. . . . Your mom's gone to Dixie and . . . What are you doing here, Feather?"

"If I explain everything, will you let me get some rest?"

"Eh, yeah."

"Then wait for me to get dressed."

Cody stared back out the front of the barn. Those weren't sock prints. They were moccasin prints. Feather's moccasins.

Cody climbed up the ladder into the loft and sat on a bale of hay and looked out at the yard below.

"Cody?"

"I'm up here in the loft."

He watched the ladder until she came into view. Her hair was loose and combed straight down on both sides of her face. She wore camouflage shorts and a camouflage T-shirt. And moccasins.

"You want some fat-free pretzels for breakfast?" She offered him a large open box.

"Eh, no thanks." Cody looked her in the eyes. "What's the deal, Feather?"

"The deal is, you weren't supposed to find me."

"What do you mean?"

"I just wanted to sleep out here one night. I was going to be gone before you got out here. But I kind of got scared last night with all the thunder and lightning and didn't sleep very well. So after I went over to Eureka's to wash up this morning about daylight, I decided to come back and take a short nap."

"Stay here one night? I don't get it."

"Look, I know all of this is difficult for you to understand, growing up in the all-American, ideal Christian family like you did, but here's the story. I just didn't want to move up to Dixie. So I . . . well, I lied. . . . Big deal. Shoot me. I told my mom that your mom said I could stay with you guys for the rest of the summer."

"You told her that?"

"Yeah. She wanted to leave early this morning, so I packed some things on my bike and told her good-bye last night. Then I rode off to town like I was coming to your house, but I came out here instead."

"You were just going to live out here all summer?"

"No, not here. I was headed back to my place this morning after mom had left."

"But—but," Cody stammered, "what about basketball . . . and all?"

"I was going to tell you that my mother allowed me to stay by myself for a few weeks and kind of wing it from there."

"Live alone?"

"Hey, I can take care of myself!"

"Is that why you had the door locked and couldn't get any sleep last night?"

"I was just a little nervous, that's all. I'll be all right once I get used to it."

"But what about food and money and stuff?"

"Yeah, well, I have some things at home, and I was sort of counting on getting that check from the commercial and—"

"Wow! I have it! I almost forgot." He pulled out the folded envelope and shoved it into her hands. "Mom called me about an hour ago and said it was in. I rode my bike out to your place to try to catch you, but everything's locked up tight."

"She's gone already? Then I can go home now." Feather tore into the envelope. "Wow! Look at this!" She flashed a check in Cody's direction.

"It's $250? I thought it was only going to be $50."

"That's what they told me . . ." She read the letter with

the check. "They have some more forms for me to sign. But they decided to give me a $250 advance instead of $50."

"Advance?"

"Yes, if they use the commercial with me in it, I get money every time it's shown. This is an advance on that money."

"Eh, whatever." Cody shrugged. "But I'm glad you got your money. What are you going to do now?"

"Go home."

"But you can't stay there, Feather. It's not safe. What about . . . you know . . . that cougar?"

"I haven't seen him around for over a week."

"But what about wackos and weirdos?"

"In north-central Idaho?"

"They're everywhere. And drunks, and pot-heads, and guys on crack and crank. A thirteen-year-old girl can't live alone."

"It might only be for a couple of weeks. Mom's coming back to check on things then . . . I think."

"But—but . . ." Cody searched for some unfailing logic. "You just can't do it, that's all. I won't allow it!"

"You? You won't allow it? Who in the world do you think you are, Cody Wayne Clark? What gives you the right to tell me what to do with my life?"

"Eh, it's the Code, Feather," Cody stammered.

The anger in the eyes began to soften. "What do you mean, it's the code?"

"The Code of the West."

"I never heard of it."

"Well, since the early days in the West, there are unwritten rules that good people try to live by."

"But that old code died out a hundred years ago—didn't it?"

"Not for some families. For me, next to the Bible, it's the most important guide for how to treat people."

"Just how do I fit into this antiquated system of chauvinistic injunctions?"

"Huh?"

"What does your code say about me?"

"Well, that it's the role of good men to protect all women and children, even with their life, if necessary."

"Which am I—a woman or a child?"

Cody felt his face flush red. He turned away. "Someplace in between, I reckon."

"And are you going to protect me?" She meant to scoff, but it came out flat.

"I'd try." He turned back to face her and found her staring right at his eyes. She didn't seem nearly as self-confident as before. He could see tears welling up in the corners of her eyes.

"You would, wouldn't you?"

"Yep."

Feather walked over and plopped down on a bale of hay next to him and stared out at the corrals. "Cody Clark, you are ruining my life. You know that, don't you?"

"What did I do?"

"All my life I've been taught how horrible the stereotyped roles for girls and boys are in our country. I've been told how the evils of society are mainly due to the decisions

118 • STEPHEN BLY

of insensitive men who lord it over women. I've been told the most destructive kind of relationship any girl can have is to be stuck with one of these guys."

"You have?"

"Yeah. And then what happens? Cody Wayne Clark comes sauntering along—"

"Saunter? Do I really saunter?"

"Hush up."

"Yes, ma'am."

"You come along, openly happy about being exactly the kind of guy that I've been warned about. It makes me so angry!"

"I don't mean to rile you."

"Would you stop being nice so I can get mad at you," she huffed.

"Yes, ma'am."

"Anyway, you come along, and you treat me just the way I was warned. This is what I've been trying to get at— I like being treated like this. I know I'm not supposed to, but I do."

"You do?"

"Yeah, and if you ever tell anyone I said that, I'll bust every tooth in your head." Feather looked away and wiped the back of her hand across her eyes.

They stared out at the yard for several minutes without talking.

Lord, I don't know what's best for Feather. It just seems like she ought to be allowed to settle down in one place long enough to grow up. If You've got any suggestions, let me know.

Feather spoke again, softly this time. "Last night I was really scared. It wasn't just the storm either. Last week when we all stayed out here, I wasn't scared at all. But now I know that was because you and the guys were up in the loft. What am I going to do, Cody?"

"I was just talking to the Lord about that."

"But you prayed about it already. I don't think God pays much attention to people like me."

"That's not true. It's just . . . I don't think you gave Him enough time."

"Are you saying I blew it?"

"Well, I don't think it was exactly His plan for you to lie to your mom and live by yourself in the tepee."

"Oh, great. The first time in my life I had anyone praying for me, and I messed it up."

The first time?

"God's able to work even if we mess things up. He's made a career out of straightening up our messes."

"So what should I do?"

"Start by telling the truth. Let's go see my mom and tell her the truth—that you lied and told your mom you were staying with us, and now you're too scared to live alone."

"I can't admit that."

"Feather, if you want the Lord to work in your life, you have to do things His way. That's how it works. And lying is not His way."

"Oh, sure, your mom's really going to want to let me stay after she hears what a liar I am."

"Nobody's perfect. But Mom always appreciates it

when I tell her the truth. I know she'll let you stay until we can figure something out."

"Really? She won't be totally ticked? I could pay her some rent for the room or something. I have this money, you know."

"I can guarantee that she won't let you pay anything for room and board."

"Why not?"

"It's part of the Code. You never turn down a person who needs something to eat or someplace to sleep. Especially if that person is a . . . a—"

"A woman or a girl?" she teased. "Which were you going to say?"

Cody leaned his head back and stared at the top of the high barn ceiling. He sighed deeply. "Uh, a young lady," he finally replied.

"You snaked out of that one, Cody Wayne." For the first time all morning, her eyes relaxed and she smiled ear to ear.

"Come on, let's bundle up your things and talk to Mom."

"You really think she'll let me stay with you guys?"

"Yep."

By noon Feather had unpacked her belongings in Prescott Clark's seldom-used upstairs bedroom.

By 1:00 P.M. it was starting to feel like home.

Nine

✦

"Well, if it isn't the Lewis and Clark Squid!" J. J. Melton growled.

After spending an hour Sunday afternoon at the Halt Historical Museum, Cody, Larry, Jeremiah, and Feather had ridden their bikes toward the Treat and Eat. An older model dark blue Ford pickup with a smashed left fender had pulled directly across the road and blocked their path.

"Squad. It's the Lewis and Clark Squad," Feather corrected.

"And what are you?" Devin asked. "The Squid Squaw?"

"You better back off, Melton," Larry warned. "My dad won't be too happy about this scene."

"Well, if it isn't Larry the Lip." As always Rocky was wearing a tank top so that all could admire his flying eagle tattoo. "What if we think you're fakin' it? What do you do then?"

"Yeah." J. J. looked straight ahead at Cody. "We're callin' your bluff, Clark. You've got one comin', and today is payday."

"Who's driving the pickup?" Jeremiah asked.

Devin glanced over at him. "Me."

"You have a driver's license?"

"I'll have it by the end of summer. That's when I turn fifteen. You want to make something of it?"

"Oh, not me." Jeremiah shook his head. "But here comes Marshal Arnett, and I've got a feeling that parking across the middle of the street might be almost as serious as driving without a license. What do you think, Cody?"

All three accusers dove into the pickup and spun gravel as they roared down the alley behind the old Liberty Theater building that now housed Ophelia's Second Hand and Antiques (closed).

"Nice thinking, Townie!" Cody slapped his hands.

"Where's the marshal?" Feather asked. "I don't see a cop car."

"The big, old green Buick. It's his wife's car." Jeremiah waved as a blonde-haired woman cruised by.

"That's Marshal Arnett?"

"Actually it's his wife," Jeremiah admitted. "But it could have been him."

"Hey, it worked. Thanks, Townie," Cody added. "Come on, let's go get a Mountain Dew at the Treat and Eat."

"Aren't you afraid of running across J. J. and the others?" Larry asked.

"I'm hoping they won't try anything in a crowd. But I guess it's just like riding a horse. You're going to get bucked off sooner of later."

"I'm not getting bucked off again," Larry insisted. "I have retired from my equestrian career."

"You?" Jeremiah asked.

"I'm never riding another horse."

"Well, in that case, I'll race all of you to the drive-in!" Jeremiah stomped on the pedals of his mountain bike as he led the quartet east on Domingo Street.

Cody, Larry, and Feather followed in leg-cramping pursuit for half a block. Then the others dropped back and left Cody to challenge Jeremiah. By changing the gears and cutting over the sidewalk at the corner of Fourth and Domingo, Cody caught up with him at the little brick building with its faded hand-printed sign TV Repair (closed). By the time they bounced into the parking lot of the Treat and Eat, the race was dead even.

Larry and Feather waited for them on the concrete bench in front of the drive-in. Her nose pointed slightly in the air.

"How did you get here?" Cody puffed.

"We won." She smiled.

Jeremiah dropped his bike to the ground in a pant. "But how did you get here?"

"Larry knew a shortcut," Feather reported.

"A shortcut? What shortcut?" Cody demanded. "I've lived here all my life, and I don't know any shortcut."

"Tough. You lose, Clark." Larry grinned, his unparted blond hair hanging straight down almost to his eyes.

Sprawled around the corner booth, all four dallied with the ice in their chartreuse-colored sodas.

"I guess we didn't learn too much today," Cody began.

"I learned that Sunday school and church wasn't nearly as bad as I imagined," Feather announced.

"Really? Hey, that's great! I guess what I meant was, we didn't learn much at the museum."

Larry blew bubbles in his Mountain Dew. "Did you hear that? I just played the theme to Sports Center. Really! Incredible, huh?"

"There's no one in the world like you, Larry," Cody agreed.

"Yeah, isn't it something? Anyway, I learned that Cougar Canyon was named after all the cougars that live there," Larry confirmed.

"Big deal. Everyone knew that." Jeremiah finished his drink, filled his straw with crushed ice, and then blew it across the table at Larry.

He missed.

"Maybe," Feather continued, "but it used to be called Stinking Water Canyon. Its name was changed right after the Italians gave up homesteading and the Bureau of Land Management took the property back."

"You're right!" Cody sat up and pulled the straw out of his drink, laid it on the table, and took a big gulp. "Cougars . . . cougars. What if that little girl was killed by cougars? Wouldn't you have a tendency to call the place Cougar Canyon after that?"

"Are you saying that maybe the C on that note in the rifle may have to do with killing cougars?" Larry asked.

Cody nodded. "Yeah, maybe."

"But what does that have to do with 'God is just'?" Feather quizzed.

"Eh . . . nothing in the world. Why is it this subject always gives me a headache?" Cody complained.

"You know what I'm tying to figure out?" Jeremiah slicked back his black butch haircut with the palm of his hand.

"What?" Cody tried to see what Yellowboy was staring at, at the far end of the cafe.

"I'm wondering what that girl's name is and why in the world I've never seen her before. Talk about an awesome smile!"

All four heads pivoted to the south end of the drive-in. A nicely tanned girl with long jet-black hair stood at the cash register holding a Gordo Grande swirl cone.

"I've never seen her. She's probably just a tourist passing through," Cody suggested.

"How come someone like that never transfers into our class?" Jeremiah continued.

"Boy, isn't that the truth," Cody mumbled and stared at the girl. "The last girl to transfer in weighed 200 pounds and had a black belt in karate."

"You guys are disgusting!" Feather growled.

"I agree. They act as if they've never seen a dynamite-looking girl in pink shorts before. Undoubtedly she's Miss Junior High Indiana out here to shoot a commercial with Bruce Baxter," Larry proposed.

Feather moaned, "This is pathetic!"

"I think her name must be Suzanne," Jeremiah suggested.

Cody shook his head. "Brittany. That's my guess."

"You must be kidding. Her name's got to be Candi. C-a-n-d-i," Larry contended.

"I'm going to puke. No kidding. This is so bad I'm going to barf all over the table!" Feather threatened. Then she jumped to her feet.

"What are you doing?" Cody whispered.

"Hey, girl with the big swirl cone," Feather shouted. Everyone in the Treat and Eat turned to stare at their table.

"Feather, sit down!" Larry commanded.

"Listen," she continued to holler, "these three jerks want to know your name. But if I were you, I wouldn't tell them because they're liable to do something extremely stupid. You know what I mean?"

Oh, no. She didn't do that. I'm not here. This isn't happening to me. Cody slipped down in the booth until his head was below the upholstered Naugahyde cushion, only to discover Larry and Jeremiah were already hiding.

It was a sweet, firm voice that replied. "Well, if you see those three jerks again, tell them my name is Lanni DeLira."

The closing of the door coincided with the crash of Cody's head into the bottom side of the cafe table.

"DeLira!" he mumbled, rubbing his head and combing his shaggy dark brown hair with his fingers.

His words were drowned out as everyone in the Treat and Eat roared with laughter. Cody wondered if he could crawl out a window at the back of the cafe instead of walking through the crowd to the front door.

Keeping low so that he wouldn't have to look at anyone other than those at his table, he leaned the back of his head against the green seat cushion.

"I can't believe you did that!" Larry groaned.

"DeLira! I can't believe she's a DeLira. Just like out at Cougar Canyon. We ought to chase her down and ask her if she's related," Feather suggested.

"Oh, sure, you expect us to chase after her with all these people watching us now?" Jeremiah chided.

"I bet it was L-a-n-n-i. With an i, right? I could just tell her name ended in an i. Am I good, or am I good?" Larry beamed.

"Where did she go? Was she walking someplace, or what?" Cody questioned.

"Yeah, she walked out and got into a red minivan with Colorado license plates," Feather acknowledged. "Of course, none of you would know that. It's hard to look out the window when your head's under the table."

"Let's go ride around town and see if we can find her," Jeremiah suggested.

"I'm not walking down that aisle until all these people leave the cafe!" Cody maintained.

"Come on, Clark, red's a good color on you. If you can figure how to stay that way, we might let you become an honorary member of the tribe," Jeremiah teased.

"If we go cruising around town, we're liable to run into J. J., Rocky, and Devin," Cody warned.

"Hey, I thought you said not to worry about that," Feather reminded him. "Which are you more scared of—finding J. J. or finding Miss Awesome DeLira?"

"We've got to ask her about Cougar Canyon," Cody

insisted. He stood to his feet and refused to look at any of the people in the cafe. "'Yea, though I walk through the valley of the shadow of death, I will fear no evil . . . '"

"What are you mumbling about, Clark?" Feather asked.

Cody marched out of the Treat and Eat without looking to the left or right. He mounted his bike and rode straight down Fourth Street until he reached Emma's Service Station and Garage (open). All four stopped on the corner.

"Man, I was never so glad to leave a place! I am never, ever going back to the Treat and Eat for the rest of my life," Cody asserted.

"Everybody in town will know about it by supper time." Jeremiah spoke with a lifetime of experience.

"Boy, is that all the thanks I get?" Feather inserted.

"Thanks?" Larry gasped. "You made us look like complete geeks."

"You were acting like complete geeks."

"Yeah, but nobody needed to know it but you," Jeremiah said.

She wrinkled her nose and twisted her long brown hair around her fingers. "I wanted to share the joy. Besides, we wouldn't have known there are DeLiras in town if I hadn't asked."

"It doesn't help if we don't know where they are."

"Let's split up and blitz town," Cody suggested. "We're looking for a red minivan with Colorado plates, right?"

"Yeah," Feather agreed. "I couldn't tell how many people were in the van."

"Townie, you and Larry cover the east side of Halt. Feather and I will divide up the west side."

"What are we going to say if we find the van?" Larry asked.

Cody stared at the two other boys for a moment.

Finally, Feather broke in. "Tell her you're one of the jerks in the cafe, and you want to know if she's related to any of the DeLiras that used to live out at Cougar Canyon."

Cody nodded agreement. "Yeah, well . . . something like that anyway."

"And what do we say if we run across J. J., Rocky, and Devin?" Jeremiah asked.

"Oh, that's easy." Larry grinned. "I'll just tell them Cody's over on the other side of town!"

"If you spot the minivan, come get us, and we'll all go talk to them together."

"Maybe we could just send Feather to talk to them," Jeremiah suggested.

"What!" she exclaimed. "Don't you want to see Miss Awesome Smile again?"

"Only from a distance—a very long distance." Jeremiah sighed.

It doesn't take long to search every street in Halt, Idaho. And a new red minivan is not easy to hide where old pickups rule. Within ten minutes the quartet met back at Emma's.

"Well, the bad news is, we didn't see the minivan," Cody reported.

"And the good news is—" Jeremiah grinned. "—we didn't see J. J. and those guys either."

"You know, if I were a DeLira," Feather proposed, "there wouldn't be anything in Halt that I would particularly want to see. But I would want to stop by that tiny graveyard."

"Right!" Cody shouted. "Let's ride out there!"

"On horseback?"

Cody looked at the panic in Larry's eyes. "No, on our bikes."

"And then we can swing out to your barn and have a practice, okay?" Larry offered.

Feather and Jeremiah nodded their approval. "Right. Practice at the ranch."

"I'll go get my basketball," Larry put in. "Then I'll meet you guys out at Cougar Canyon."

"We can wait, Larry—if you want us to," Cody replied.

"Hey, no sweat. I'll just take the gravel road out behind the rodeo grounds and turn left at the T, correct?"

"Yep," Jeremiah replied.

"I've got a great new play I invented last night. Feather will steal the ball from them at the top of the key and—"

"I like it already." She beamed.

"Save it, Larry. Tell us when we get out to the barn. If we don't hurry, there won't be any way of catching up with the DeLiras," Cody insisted.

The scattered clouds that had sailed over Halt most of the day had now backed up against the Bitterroot

Mountains to the east. Cody knew there was a good chance of another summer storm during the night—or sooner. The road to the rodeo grounds was fairly wide and hard-packed from heavy use, but beyond the arena, the road narrowed, and the gravel ceased. It was no more than two worn ruts at the edge of a hay field next to tribal-owned timber.

Jeremiah pulled up alongside him.

Cody pointed to the tracks in the dirt roadway. "Someone's driven down here since the last storm."

"You think they're fresh?" Jeremiah asked.

"Can't tell. I don't see any animal tracks or anything disturbing the prints, but I don't know if there are many animals out this way."

"Are you guys sure this road leads to Cougar Canyon? I thought it was more toward the Clark ranch," Feather asked.

"It is," Cody replied, "but you have to swing out to the east and then come back on the ridge of Porcupine Point to get there from here."

"Porcupine Point!" Jeremiah teased. "Whew! You want me to drop back and leave you two alone on Porcupine Point?"

"Townie!" It came out sounding more like a threat than a nickname.

"What are you talking about?" Feather called up to them.

"Nothing!" Cody huffed.

"Is this the first time you ever took a girl to Porcupine Point?" Jeremiah continued to razz Cody.

"What are you guys talking about?" she demanded.

"Yellowboy, you are about to shorten your life span by seventy-five years!" Cody growled and sped on out ahead of the other two.

"What's that all about?" Feather asked, pumping hard to stay up with Jeremiah.

"You've heard about Porcupine Point, haven't you? Everybody in high school talks about it. Oh, yeah, you're home-schooled. Well, it's one of those places where the guys bring their girlfriends and . . . you know . . . it has a great view of the canyon."

"I wonder how long this awkward stage lasts in boys?" She rubbed the back of her hand across her cheek smearing a little red road dust like rouge.

Cody figured it took close to an hour to bike to the head of Cougar Canyon. It looked different coming in from the east. With fifty-year-old second-growth timber and matted green brush scattered down the canyon draw, it was difficult for him to imagine the place as a homestead. Car tracks in the dirt caught his eye.

"We missed them! Looks like the car stopped here, and several people got out and hiked down to the graves."

Jeremiah leaned forward across his handlebars. "They're probably on their way back wherever home is."

Feather climbed off her bike and let it drop to the dirt. "Let's go down and look at the grave. Maybe they left a clue."

"Oh, sure—a nice little 'To Whom It May Concern' note with a complete family history," Cody kidded.

Feather stuck out her tongue and traipsed on down to the opening in the bramble that Cody had made on Thursday.

"Cody, my man, we aren't ever going to see that awesome smile again," Jeremiah sighed.

"I was just hoping we could find out about that note in your grandad's rifle," Cody answered.

"Yeah, that's the only reason I wanted to catch up with the minivan, too." Jeremiah's grin hung like a drooping clothesline between his ears.

"You're disgusting—both of you," Feather stewed.

Jeremiah giggled. "Thank you."

She let go of a branch that would have caught Cody in the face if he hadn't ducked. "I was right. There is a clue!" she shouted.

When Cody broke into the clearing, Feather held a folded sheet of yellow note paper. "Where did you get that? What is it?"

"It was on top of this stone, held in place by a rock."

"What does it say?" Jeremiah implored.

"It's a note for me," she announced, holding it pressed tight against her chest.

"What do you mean, for you?"

"It begins: 'To the one who placed the wildflowers on the grave.' That's me."

"What else does it say?"

"I should tell you? You're the two who scoffed at my idea that there would be a clue at the grave."

"Okay, you were right. We were wrong," Cody admitted. "What does it say?"

She held the note off to her side so they couldn't read it. "It says: 'Please tell the cute boy in the black sleeveless T-shirt to meet me at Porcupine Point at 7:00 P.M. tonight.' Signed, Lanni 'Awesome-Smile' DeLira."

Jeremiah lunged without success at the paper.

"It doesn't say that!" Cody exclaimed and snatched the note from her hand. Feather kicked him in the shin. He staggered back and dropped the note.

"Ow!" he squealed.

"It's my note."

Cody rubbed his lower leg. "Feather," he panted, "may we please read the note that was left to you?"

"Why didn't you say that in the first place?" She handed Jeremiah the note.

He read out loud: "'To the one who placed the wild-flowers on the grave: Thank you for your kindness. Sincerely, the DeLira Family.'"

"That's it?" Cody was still rubbing his shin. "No names, no address—"

"Not even a telephone number!" Feather folded the note and put it in the pocket of her cut-off jeans. "Come on, romeos. It's time for basketball practice."

Reaching the bikes, Cody stared back down the trail to the east.

"You looking for Larry?" Feather asked.

"Yeah. I figured he'd catch up by now."

"You think he went straight out to the ranch?" Jeremiah asked.

"Maybe." Cody grabbed a stick and wrote something in the dirt.

Feather leaned closer. "What are you doing?"

"Leaving Larry a note."

Jeremiah stretched his arms behind his head. "We could just wait here. We can't play basketball until Larry shows up anyway."

"Yeah, but we can get a drink at Eureka's!" Feather stated.

"You guys want to race to the ranch?" Jeremiah challenged.

"Nope," Cody replied.

"Not me," Feather added.

"Good. I didn't want to either."

When they reached County Line Road, they spotted Larry pedaling toward the Clark ranch. They waited for him at the corner.

"Hey, guys," Larry hollered as he approached, "you didn't have trouble with J. J. and the others, did you?"

"We didn't see them," Jeremiah reported.

"Well, they just roared into town from this direction. I thought they might try to hassle me or something, but they flew on by."

"What do you think they were doing out here?" Feather wondered.

"Just looking for Cody, I suppose."

Cody rode ahead of the others as they took the gravel road up to the ranch. *Lord, I'm really, really getting tired of this. But I don't know what to do. Whatever's supposed to happen next, could it hurry up and happen?*

He turned toward the barn and parked his bike next to the loading chute.

"Whoa!" Jeremiah gasped.

Feather's voice sounded surprised. "This is not a good sign."

"Just how are we going to practice now?" Larry moaned.

Cody glanced up at the side of the barn.

There was no backboard.

No basket.

No rim.

No net.

Nothing.

Nothing but four empty bolt holes in the barn board.

Ten

✳

"Did you tell Marshall Arnett about J. J. stealing your backboard?" Larry quizzed.

Cody tossed another loop around the plastic steer head and squinted into the early morning sun. "No, we didn't really see J. J. take it. Besides, my dad said he figures it was just a prank, and it will show up soon. We only call the sheriff's office for matters we can't handle ourselves. And he figures we can handle this."

"Some more of that 'life on the western frontier' stuff?"

"Yep." Cody built a loop and swung it over his head.

"Where's Jeremiah and Feather?"

"Townie's eating breakfast, and Feather, well, I guess she likes to sleep in. I think it's been awhile since she had her own bed and her own room."

"Hey, Cody!" Jeremiah Yellowboy bolted out the back door of the Clark home barefoot, a rolled-up pancake in one hand. "Mr. Weston, the park manager, just called. He heard down at the coffee shop that you were missing a backboard and hoop."

"Yeah?"

"Well, he said there's one floating out in the middle of Expedition Lake."

"What?"

"He said we could borrow one of their rowboats if we want to go out there and haul it in."

"They tossed it in the lake?" Larry sputtered.

"Let's go get it!" Cody shouted. "Get your shoes, Townie, and wake up Feather. She might want to go."

"Why don't you wake her up?" Jeremiah protested.

"Hey, it's no big deal."

"Good. Then you do it."

Cody sighed.

He gently tapped on Feather's door. Hearing no response, he banged on it and called out, "Feather?"

"Well, come in," she replied. "Don't stand out there beating on my door."

"Eh, I can't. Listen, we're going over to the lake to—"

"What do you mean, you can't?"

"I can't go into a girl's room. Anyway, my backboard's floating out in the middle of Expedition Lake, and we're—"

"That's the dumbest thing I ever heard," she shouted back through the closed door.

"Yeah, it is kind of strange that it showed up in the lake, but we can—"

"No! What kind of rule is it that says you can't come into a girl's room?"

"My mother said it isn't proper because—"

"Even if the girl says it's okay?"

"Eh, if the girl opens the door and leaves it open, then it's all right to step inside."

"Brother!" Feather sighed.

Cody heard her pad over to the door and swing it open. He peeked inside. She was completely dressed, had the bed made, and the room neat and orderly.

"I thought maybe you were sleeping in."

"I was reading," she announced. "Now what's this about the lake?"

"What were you reading?" Cody thought he saw one of Prescott's black Bibles lying open on the dresser.

"Oh, just one of your brother's books. He sure does underline a lot. Now what's this about the backboard?"

"It's floating in the middle of the lake. Townie, Larry, and I are going to go get it. You want to go?"

"You mean, swim out there?"

"No, we'll take a rowboat. The park manager said we could borrow one of his."

"I'll change my shoes and be right out."

He stepped back out and pulled the door closed.

"Cody?" she called from inside.

"Yeah?"

"Hey, I like that rule—about a girl's room."

"Yeah," he replied, "so do I."

Expedition Lake was at one time just a meadow high in the mountains, surrounded by majestic ponderosa pine trees. At the turn of the century, a lumber mill opened on the creek, and the meadow turned into a mill pond. It was named Expedition Lake in honor of the Lewis and Clark Expedition of 1805 and 1806. But after the mill shut down, the lake was taken over by the State Parks and Recreation Department. Now it's ringed with campgrounds, picnic areas, and fishermen.

Too small for motorboats but stocked with trout, bass, and catfish, it's a popular summer destination for families—and now basketball backboards.

Cody barked out the orders. "Feather, you sit up front. Larry gets in the back, and me and Townie will row. Hey! Take it easy. We don't want to capsize this sucker before we get away from the dock."

The clouds stacked up in the east. Even though it was nearly sixty degrees, the wind off the water felt cold on Cody's bare arms. He was glad he wore jeans instead of shorts.

"Did you know me and Cody have won the Expedition Lake Rowboat Race twice?" Jeremiah declared.

"What's that?" Larry asked.

"Every summer during the Halt Fourth of July Days, they have rowboat races for different age groups. Well, me and Cody were champs in our age bracket twice. We could have won three times in a row if it hadn't been for that big water fight."

"Who did you get into a water fight with?" Larry queried.

"Each other." Cody grinned. "I thought we were going to sink the boat there for a while."

"How in the world can you get into a water fight with each other in the same boat?" Feather asked.

Cody glanced over at Jeremiah, who nodded his head in agreement. In unison the boys skimmed their paddles forward across the surface of the lake, sending a spray of water onto Feather from both sides.

"Oh!" she shrieked, jumping straight up to her feet. As she did, the boat began to rock wildly back and forth.

"Whoa!" Jeremiah called.

"Watch out! Sit down!" Larry hollered from the back of the boat where he clutched the sides with both hands.

"I'm soaked!" Feather complained as she tried to regain her balance. She wiped the water out of her eyes, and in doing so, she staggered back and tripped over the seat.

Cody dropped the oar in the water and dove for Feather, tackling her around the knees. She sat back down on the front bench seat with a bang and a splash. He raised up his head but still clutched her legs. The palm of her right hand struck his left cheek with a resounding crack. He jerked back to the right with such force that again the boat nearly capsized.

"Sit down!" Larry called out. "Sit down!"

Cody slunk back into his seat next to Jeremiah, fished the paddle out of the lake, and then rubbed his cheek.

"Well," Feather replied, "I see how people could get in a tiff in the same rowboat."

They paddled for a few more yards without anyone talking.

Finally she glanced back at Cody. "Sorry I slapped you so hard. I was mad and didn't plan on clobbering you quite like that."

"It's okay. I didn't know we were going to drown you. It's kind of hard to gauge how much water to splash. I thought you were going to fall in—really."

"I was."

"Then we're friends again?" he asked.

"Friends?" Feather crossed her arms and scowled. "We are more than friends, and you know it!"

"We are?" He could feel his throat swelling into a lump.

"Yeah," Larry blurted out, "you're teammates! The Lewis and Clark Squad. Remember? Hey, you know what we could do? We could enter the rowboat race this year as a team. Wouldn't that be cool?"

"Put your hand in the water, Larry," Jeremiah instructed.

"Whoa! It's cold!" Larry shivered.

"Yeah. That's how cool it would be if we were all on the same rowboat team."

Cody was happy to see his backboard floating with the hoop up. He tossed his rope around the orange rim and dallied it off to the back of the boat. It was much slower paddling back to the boat ramp.

Feather sat in the front but faced backwards. Her tie-dyed T-shirt showed the results of the water fight. Cody kept glancing back to make sure the backboard was in tow.

"Hey, am I just imagining things, or is that a red mini-van parked near the boat ramp?" Larry cried.

"Full speed ahead, Townie," Cody shouted.

"Aye-aye, Captain Clark!" Jeremiah laughed.

Making it to shore with the boat was the easy part. Dragging the water-logged backboard to dry land proved to be difficult. All four tugged on the rope, finally dragging it up on the bank next to a picnic table.

"Now what?" Feather asked. "You did notice that the minivan has Colorado license plates, didn't you?"

"But I don't see them anywhere," Cody replied.

"No."

"Maybe they hiked around to the back of the lake," Jeremiah suggested.

"Yeah . . . well," Cody pondered. "Let's . . . I'll go find someone to bring a rig back here and load up the backboard. Townie, why don't you hike around to the back of the lake and see if the DeLiras are there. Larry, you search the nature trail, and, Feather, you wait by the backboard so someone doesn't steal it or shove it back into the water."

"Oh, sure, make me baby-sit the backstop while you guys look for Miss Awesome Smile."

"Hey. I'll sit by the backstop," Larry offered. "I don't like nature trails."

"Why?" Jeremiah asked.

"Too many bugs," Larry explained. "I mean, I'm . . . sort of allergic to bug bites."

Cody jogged most of the way back around the lake and up to his house. Denver was home but on the telephone talking to Becky. Cody had time to eat an extra-sharp cheddar cheese and dill pickle sandwich and read the first six pages of the current issue of *ProRodeo Sports News* before his big brother hung up the phone and agreed to load up the backboard.

By the time they reached the marina, Jeremiah and Feather were sitting on a park bench watching Larry draw something in the dirt.

"Hi, Denver!" Feather called out.

"Hey, lil' sis. That might be the biggest catch anyone ever made in Expedition Lake." He pointed at the backboard.

"I'm glad you finally made it," Jeremiah groaned. "Larry was making us memorize six new plays for tonight's game."

"Cody, come look. This will blow them away. I saw UMass use it against Georgetown!" Larry insisted.

Ignoring Larry, Cody helped his brother lift the dripping wet wooden backboard into the back of the truck.

"The minivan's gone," he noted. "Did you find the DeLiras?"

"Yes . . . and no." Feather scowled.

"What do you mean?"

"Well, they weren't in the campground, and I didn't find them on the nature trail."

"I guess they were back at the old bridge," Jeremiah replied.

"So you didn't see them?"

"We didn't, but Larry did," Jeremiah said.

"No kidding? All right, Larry, what did she say?"

"I think Prince Charming was at a loss for words," Feather sneered.

"You did talk to her, didn't you? You told her we were the ones who put the flowers on the grave and cleared the brush? I mean, you did ask if they knew anything about the gun and the riddle and—"

"Eh . . . not really." Larry bit down on his lip and tugged at the shirttail of the Indiana Pacers T-shirt. "Did you know she has the longest black eyelashes I've ever seen?"

"She what? Larry . . . didn't you talk to her at all?"

"Oh, sure. I told her you were looking for her."

"Me!" Cody choked. "We were all looking for her."

"Yeah, that's what I meant, but it just came out that you were looking for her. And then I said—"

"I can't believe this! " Cody fumed as they crowded into the back of his brother's pickup. Feather hopped into the cab next to Denver. "We've been looking all over for them, and all you can say is, 'Cody is looking for you'?"

"Look, I was a little nervous. I'm not used to talking to girls like you are."

Cody glanced over at Larry, who was looking down at his basketball shoes the whole time. "Hey, no big deal. I probably wouldn't have done any better," he admitted. "And don't ever think I'm good at talking to girls."

"Well, you and Feather are always visiting and—"

"Yeah, but Feather doesn't really act like a girl. She's easy to talk to."

"Do you want to hear what else I told Lanni DeLira?"

"You said something else?"

"Yeah, I invited her to our basketball game."

"You did what?"

"She and her folks and grandmother are staying at McCurley's Bed and Breakfast. She said she'd see if they'd let her come up to the gym and watch the game. I told her you'd talk with her then."

"Me?"

"Yeah, I knew you'd want to question her."

"About what?"

"About the gun and the note and the grave and the riddle."

"Oh . . . yeah . . . that." For the first time all day Cody was beginning to feel very nervous about the game.

"Actually I'm getting used to these uniforms," Larry admitted as he tucked in his tie-dyed shirt. "Not that I want to wear them all summer, but just the same, they are unique."

Cody sat on the bleachers retying his shoes even though they didn't need it. "Why don't you tell Feather that?"

"I'm afraid she'll go out and make us some more. Know what I mean? I really think we're going to win tonight. Mom fixed my lucky meatloaf. Where is Feather anyway?"

"She said she needed to take more time to get ready. I guess she heard Denver and my folks are coming to watch us."

"She acts like a moon-dork around Denver sometimes."

"You ought to see her at our house. She can be a real pest!"

"How about Jeremiah?"

"Oh, he's cool."

"No," Larry persisted, "where is he?"

"He was still waiting for a phone call from his mother. He'll be right over."

"Oh, great. Look who else is going to watch!" Larry's eyes followed three boys entering the gym.

"J. J., Rocky, and Devin." Cody sighed.

"They don't have a game tonight. Maybe they came to scout us out. See, I told you that we had them worried."

"They probably came to see what kind of reaction we had to them tossing my backboard into the lake."

"Here comes the whole gang."

Cody glanced up to see Feather, Jeremiah, Denver, and his parents.

The Lewis and Clark Squad shot around and practiced a couple of drills while the bleachers gradually filled up.

"Do you see her yet?" Cody asked.

Feather stole the ball from him and drove to the hoop. "Who?"

"You know . . . Lanni."

"Yes, I know!" Feather wrinkled her nose. "Are you sure you're going to be able to concentrate on the game?"

Cody glanced back at the double doors that led to the entry hall. "Oh, sure . . . eh, what did you say?"

Feather turned to Larry. "Cody's a little fuzzy tonight. Better keep an eye on him, coach."

"I am not! Hey, Townie, here come your brothers!"

"All right! Let's do it!" Jeremiah shouted.

Larry, Cody, and Jeremiah opened the game. The Loggers ricocheted a three-point shot off the front rim, and

Cody pulled down the rebound. He bounced the ball out to Larry, who fired it to Jeremiah and then broke to the basket. A quick pass to Cody, then a fake shot followed by a drop-off to the slashing Larry Bird Lewis. It was an easy bucket.

This time the Loggers' three-pointer recoiled off the backboard and into the net. The Squad followed this with the same play as earlier, only this time Cody skipped the ball back out to Jeremiah, who fired up a three-pointer.

Nothing but net.

Cody watched as Jeremiah scanned the audience for his brothers. They flashed thumbs up.

"There she is!" Cody shouted.

"Where?" Larry asked.

"Down in front of J. J. Look!"

Larry was too busy guarding Dillon McClure. But it was Tater Webb who was standing by himself under the basket for the easy lay-in.

"Come on, Clark, that was your man!" he heard his brother yell from the stands.

Cody got the inbound pass from Larry and drove to the basket. He dribbled the ball off his foot, and it bounced out of bounds.

I can't believe I did that! He glanced back toward Lanni DeLira. *What's she doing talking to J. J.?*

"Cody!" He glanced up just in time to see the basket-ball slam into his midsection.

"What? I thought . . ."

The turn-over cost them another basket.

"Get in the game, dude!" Jeremiah hollered.

Glancing up, he noticed that DeLira was no longer sitting in the bleachers.

She went home. I don't blame her. It's pretty embarrassing.

This time he took the inbound and bounced it to Larry, who drove to the hoop. Larry's shot was off to the right, but Cody flew above the Loggers to snatch the rebound and put it right back up.

Oh, sure. Now I make one!

Larry stole the ball from McClure and tossed it to Townie. Cody moved under the basket, in position for a rebound. Instead of shooting the three, Jeremiah launched a high pass in to Cody, who leaped into the air to catch the ball. He decided to shoot while still in the air.

Off the glass and into the net.

"All right. Alley-oop!" Jeremiah hollered.

"Cody, Feather's coming in for you!" Larry yelled.

Cody ran to the bench, then froze in his tracks at the sight of Lanni DeLira sitting next to Feather.

What's she doing on our bench?

Feather dashed into the game, and Cody stumbled toward the bleachers. He felt his throat start to tighten up. He could hardly swallow. He had a sudden urge to get a drink of water—at the stock tank in Eureka Blaine's backyard.

"Hi, I'm Lanni."

"Eh . . ."

"And you're Cody, right?"

"Well, I . . ."

"Feather said I could sit with your team." Her smile

seemed to be connected with the sparkle in her eyes. Her words felt like a tickle up and down the back of his neck.

"Oh . . . then . . . I . . . well . . ."

"Hey, look at that." She pointed to the court. "Feather's really quick, isn't she?"

"I'm . . . I'm Cody," he mumbled.

"Yeah, I know," she replied. "Maybe you should sit down and watch the game."

Larry's right. Those are the longest eyelashes in the world. Sort of like one of those movie stars.

"Well?"

"Huh?"

"Are you going to sit down?"

"Oh . . . yeah."

Out on the court Larry Lewis was going wild. Jumpers. Slashes to the basket. No-look passes.

Feather stole the ball.

Jeremiah lived up to his nickname and made a couple from downtown.

And Larry did everything else.

Cody thought he heard Jeremiah call for him to come in, but he hesitated and was left sitting on the bench. In what seemed like a flash the game was over.

I'll ask her about the riddle in the rifle and the grave and maybe see if she wants to go down to the Treat and Eat for a . . . no, no, I'm never going back there.

"Whoa!" Larry hollered, and the team gathered at the bleachers. "Was I hot, or was I hot?"

"Your whole team is good, Larry." Lanni grinned.

"Where did you come up with that opening play? I saw the Wildcats do the same thing in the play-offs last year."

"You watched the play-offs?" Larry gasped.

Cody scooted in next to Lanni. *I'll ask her about that riddle.*

"Basketball is big when you grow up in Kentucky."

"You're from Kentucky?" Larry asked. "I thought you were from Colorado."

"No, we just came out to visit my grandmother in Colorado. I live in Kentucky. Just across the river from Cincinnati."

Cody figured her voice was sort of like a symphony. Expressive and melodious. *Ask her to go with the team for a Coke.*

"Hey, Clark!"

J. J., Rocky, and Devin stalked along the back edge of the bleachers.

"You done any fishin' lately?" J. J. taunted.

Okay, Lord, this is where I need some help.

"We heard you were thinkin' of takin' up water polo!" Rocky jibed.

Cody took a big, deep breath. "You guys won't believe what we pulled out of the lake."

"Oh?" Devin raised his eyebrows in mock surprise.

"My basketball backboard!"

"No foolin'?" J. J. sneered. "How do you suppose it got there?"

"Well, you tossed it in the lake."

J. J. stiffened. "You want to make somethin' of it?"

Lord, what do I do now?

"No." Cody felt himself relax. "I figure I sort of deserved something like that, didn't I?"

J. J. raised his eyebrows and looked over at Rocky and Devin. "Yeah, you did."

Denver stood a few feet away. He gave him a thumbs-up sign and then commented, "You done good all the way around, lil' bro. I'll see you at the house."

"Hey, Clark," Rocky called out, "who was that good-lookin' babe with the jet-black hair that took off with Larry 'the Dweeb' Lewis?"

"Oh, her name is Lanni, but she . . ." *Took off?*

Cody jerked around. Jeremiah was heading toward the front door of the gym with Two Ponies and Sweetwater. Feather stood behind him with her arms crossed.

"Where's Larry—and Lanni?"

"She went with our fearless captain to see his basketball card collection."

"She did what? With Larry?"

"She likes basketball. What else can I say?"

"But—but what about the gun . . . the note . . . the riddle?" he stammered.

"Come on, I'll tell you everything on the way home." She motioned for him to follow.

They cut through the city park on their way back to the Clark house, and Feather parked herself in a swing. Cody took the one next to her.

"See, while you were out there making something of a fool of yourself, I invited her to sit down with our team," Feather explained. "And I asked her about the note."

"What did she say?"

"She didn't know anything about it, but she did tell me about the grave and the 'God is just' marker. The story her grandmother told her was that they had bought the rifle to kill cougars prowling in the canyon."

"Just like Mr. Levine told us."

"A cougar killed two of their goats. Then it attacked their milk cow, but Lanni's grandfather shot and killed it with the rifle."

"But what about the grave?"

"That was for Lanni's father's little sister Dora. The gun had been stolen by then, and they didn't have any way to kill the other cougar. It attacked the children playing, and they tried to chase it off with rocks and sticks, but the little girl was so badly clawed she died."

"So they planted the trees and chiseled the grave marker?"

"Exactly."

"But what about the riddle?"

"Well, guess who stole the rifle?"

"The guy in the jail when it was blown up?"

"Yes! He had stopped by their house, and they fed him and let him sleep in the barn for a couple weeks because he was Italian. But when he left, he stole some money and the rifle. Guess what his name was."

"A. Al? Arthur? Aaron?" Cody guessed.

"Adolfo!"

"The A in the formula!" he exclaimed. "So when his friends blew up the jail on his head, they figured it was God's justice?"

"I guess so. Is that the way God works, Cody?"

"Well, we do reap what we sow. Sooner or later it will catch up with us. But if the guy stole the rifle, how did the note get in there?"

"The police found the gun and returned it to the DeLira family."

"And they shot the other cougar?"

"Yeah. But Lanni said during the war, they abandoned their claim and moved back to Kentucky to be with other family members."

Cody began swinging back and forth. "Adolfo + B . . ."

"For bomb!" Feather cried.

"C for cougars + D for Dora DeLira = God is just."

"Lanni figures maybe her grandpa put the note in the gun before he sold it back to Mr. Levine."

"You learned all of that during the basketball game?"

"That's not all I learned from Miss Awesome Smile."

"Oh?"

"I happen to know she definitely has a major crush on one member of the Lewis and Clark Squad."

"Oh, yeah?" Cody stopped swinging and looked straight at Feather's eyes. "Which one?"

"Larry." She grinned.

"You're kidding! But he doesn't even . . . He's too . . ."

Feather shook her head. "Tell me the truth, Cody. Do I act as much like a dork around Denver as you do around Lanni?"

He sighed and looked up at the clouds sailing over the blue north-central Idaho sky.

"Yep."

"That's what I figured. I'll race you home. One, two,

three, go!" Feather bolted from the swing and sprinted south across the grassy park.

Cody dashed to catch up. "That wasn't a fair start!" he complained.

"I know," Feather giggled, "but I always wanted to know what it would feel like to have a boy chase me!"

For a list of other books by Stephen Bly
or information regarding speaking engagements
write:

Stephen Bly
Winchester, Idaho 83555